NEW YORK

A Literary Anthology

More regional anthologies
from Macmillan Collector's Library

Paris: A Literary Anthology
edited by Zachary Seager

London: An Illustrated Literary Companion
edited by Rosemary Gray

Treasures of Cornwall: A Literary Anthology
edited by Luke Thompson

Yorkshire: A Literary Landscape
edited by David Stuart Davies

NEW YORK

A Literary Anthology

Edited and introduced by
J. MICHELLE COGHLAN

MACMILLAN COLLECTOR'S LIBRARY

This collection first published 2026 by Macmillan Collector's Library
an imprint of Pan Macmillan
The Smithson, 6 Briset Street, London EC1M 5NR
EU representative: Macmillan Publishers Ireland Ltd, 1st Floor,
The Liffey Trust Centre, 117–126 Sheriff Street Upper,
Dublin 1 D01 YC43
Associated companies throughout the world

ISBN 978-1-0350-6766-4

Introduction and author biographies © J. Michelle Coghlan 2026
Selection © Macmillan Publishers International Ltd 2026

The Permissions Acknowledgements on pp.197–9 constitute
an extension of this copyright page.

All rights reserved. No part of this publication may be reproduced, stored in
a retrieval system, or transmitted, in any form, or by any means (including,
without limitation, electronic, mechanical, photocopying, recording or
otherwise) without the prior written permission of the publisher.

1 3 5 7 9 8 6 4 2

Map © Library of Congress, Geography and Map Division

A CIP catalogue record for this book is available from the British Library.

Typeset in Plantin by Six Red Marbles UK, Thetford, Norfolk
Printed and bound in the UK using 100% Renewable Electricity by CPI Group (UK) Ltd

This book is sold subject to the condition that it shall not, by way of
trade or otherwise, be lent, hired out, or otherwise circulated without
the publisher's prior consent in any form of binding or cover other than
that in which it is published and without a similar condition including this
condition being imposed on the subsequent purchaser. The publisher does not
authorize the use or reproduction of any part of this book in any manner
for the purpose of training artificial intelligence technologies or systems.
The publisher expressly reserves this book from the Text and Data Mining
exception in accordance with Article 4(3) of the European Union
Digital Single Market Directive 2019/790.

Visit **www.panmacmillan.com** to read more
about all our books and to buy them.

Contents

Map x
Introduction xiii

OLD NEW YORK, LOST NEW YORK

WASHINGTON IRVING 3
from Knickerbocker's History of New York

HENRY JAMES 7
from Washington Square

LYDIA MARIA CHILD 11
from Letters from New-York

JAMES D. MCCABE 17
from The Secrets of the Great City

EDITH WHARTON 27
Mrs. Manstey's View

YUNG WING 44
from My Life in China and America

PAULE MARSHALL 46
from Brown Girl, Brownstones

ON MOVING TO NEW YORK

EMMA GOLDMAN 53
from Living My Life

W. D. HOWELLS 59
from A Hazard of New Fortunes

THEODORE DREISER 71
from Sister Carrie

JAMES WELDON JOHNSON 77
from The Autobiography of an Ex-Colored Man

ANAÏS NIN 87
Letter to Henry Miller

MISERY AND THE METROPOLIS

CHARLES DICKENS 93
from American Notes

LOUISA MAY ALCOTT 101
Letter to Her Nephews

JACOB RIIS 106
from How the Other Half Lives

STEPHEN CRANE 111
from Maggie: A Girl of the Streets

ABRAHAM CAHAN 118
from Yekl: A Tale of the New York Ghetto

MAXIM GORKY 123
from Boredom

THE POETRY OF THE CITY

WALT WHITMAN 131
Mannahatta

EMMA LAZARUS 134
The New Colossus

SARA TEASDALE 136
Broadway
The Lights of New York

EDNA ST VINCENT MILLAY 139
Recuerdo

CLAUDE MCKAY 141
The Tropics in New York
On Broadway

LANGSTON HUGHES 144
Lenox Avenue: Midnight

ELIZABETH BISHOP 146
Invitation to Miss Marianne Moore

ALLEN GINSBERG 150
My Sad Self

AUDRE LORDE 154
A Trip on the Staten Island Ferry

GRIEF AND THE CITY

DAWN POWELL 159
from A Time to Be Born

JESS ROW 163
from Nobody Ever Gets Lost

THE MAGIC OF NEW YORK

MARGARET FULLER 169
from Farewell

MARK TWAIN 172
from Mark Twain's Letters

HENRY JAMES 177
from The American Scene

DJUNA BARNES 183
Why Go Abroad?

DOROTHY PARKER 188
from My Hometown

HELEN KELLER 192
from Midstream: My Later Life

Permissions Acknowledgements 197

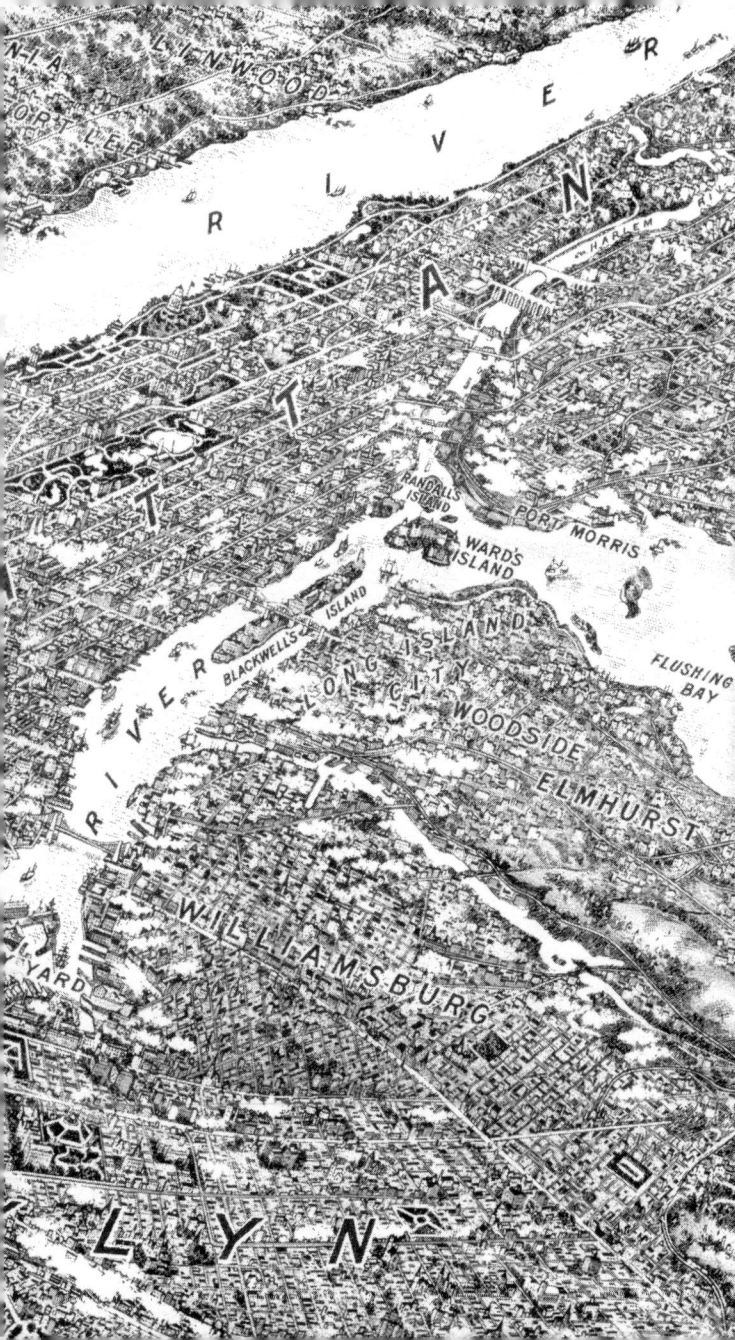

Introduction

J. MICHELLE COGHLAN

In the smash-hit musical *Hamilton*, which debuted on Broadway in 2015 and at the time of writing is still running in London at the Victoria Palace Theatre, Lin-Manuel Miranda unabashedly belts out, 'In New York, you can be a new man (just you wait)'. That iconic line is uttered by the musical's titular character, Founding Father Alexander Hamilton, shortly after his arrival in the city in 1776, but it could just as easily have popped from the mouth of Don Draper, the fantastically talented 1960s Madison Avenue ad man and master of reinvention at the centre of the critically acclaimed TV series *Mad Men*, which first aired in the US in 2007 and ran for seven seasons. That New York is a city of big dreams, endless possibilities, and – perhaps more than anywhere else in America – the place to go if you want to remake yourself is equally famously borne out in many recent pop song odes to the city, among them Taylor Swift's 'Welcome to New York' (2014) and Jay Z and Alicia Keys' 'Empire State of Mind' (2009).

The dream of exactly that sort of New York runs like a magical through line across many of the writers assembled within the pages of this literary anthology. You can hear it pulsing through the opening lines of Emma Goldman's 1931 memoir, *Living My Life*, which begins not with her birth, but instead with her arrival in the great metropolis where she first found herself as an activist, writer and speaker. As Goldman puts it, 'All that had happened in my life until that time was now left behind me, cast off like a worn-out garment. A new world was before me, strange and terrifying.' It shows up, too, in Whitman's rhapsodic views of his city's 'numberless crowded streets' in his 1860 poem 'Mannahatta'; in Sara Teasdale's evocation of 'the liquid splendor of the lights' on Broadway in her 1915 poem of that name; and in the musings of the newly arrived narrator in James Weldon Johnson's 1912 novel, *The Autobiography of an Ex-Colored Man*, who not without some trepidation begins to feel 'the dread power of the city: the crowds, the lights, the excitement, the gayety and all its subtler stimulating influences began to take effect upon me. My blood ran quicker, and I felt I was just beginning to live'. That New York is quintessentially a place for fresh starts also textures Dorothy Parker's fondness for the city she dubs her 'hometown', by choice rather than birth. As she puts it in her 1928 essay, 'I suppose that is the thing about New York. It is always a little more than you had hoped for. Each day there, is so definitely a new day. "Now we will start all over," it seems to say every morning, "and come on, let's hurry like anything."'

That so many still dream of glimpsing or being part of that New York is evident not just from the thousands who continue to move there each year, but also in the millions of visitors from around the world who make their way there as tourists. Even those of us who have never made the trip ourselves might have a taste of that dream city already in our heads: the desire to wander its streets; stroll through Central Park in autumn; see the Christmas lights at Rockefeller Center; line up for the best bagel in town; feel the crush of the crowds on Broadway; duck into a bar or cafe that an author or musician we love used to haunt, in part because New York has had so many admirers who have captured its beauties and eccentricities on camera, page and screen, in Broadway songs and hit albums, over the years.

Perhaps surprisingly, though, New York's great bards and mythologizers only came onto the scene in great numbers in the twentieth century, the decades that saw the city at the heart of a great many of the most influential literary and artistic movements of the day, including literary modernism, the Harlem Renaissance, the New York School of Poetry circle of writers, Abstract Expressionism, the Beat Generation, pop art, punk music, street art and hip-hop. For there was a distinct flip side to the dream of New York that began to take hold in the nineteenth century, a period which saw its population dramatically increase from just over 60,000 in 1800 to over 515,000 fifty years later. And by that other account, New York was more a problem to be fixed than a city of fantasy: a place of newcomers and upstarts, turbocharged business ventures, jacked-up rental prices, unbridled consumerism, overcrowded streets and dangerously overfilled tenements, bohemian artists, questionable morals, rampant crime and a hotbed of labour agitation and radical activism. As

Mark Twain put it while visiting the city in 1867, 'I have at last, after several months' experience, made up my mind that it is a splendid desert – a domed and steepled solitude, where the stranger is lonely in the midst of a million of his race . . . Every man seems to feel that he has got the duties of two lifetimes to accomplish in one, and so he rushes, rushes, rushes, and never has time to be companionable – never has any time at his disposal to fool away on matters which do not involve dollars and duty and business.' Over the course of the nineteenth century, that less quixotic side of the city came to be chronicled in a series of sensational and widely read urban exposés, philanthropic dispatches, gritty naturalist novels and, perhaps most famously, *How the Other Half Lives*, Jacob Riis's groundbreaking 1890 book of photojournalism on the crushing poverty and abject conditions in the tenements of Manhattan's Lower East Side, where roughly 240,000 people were squeezed into each square mile.

The writers assembled here tell both these stories about New York, and others besides. Washington Irving conjures the now mostly vanished Dutch New York, while Henry James lingers over memories of a New York that was more bucolic than we might now imagine Manhattan could be. Through the eyes of writers such as W. D. Howells, Theodore Dreiser and Anaïs Nin, we find ourselves in the footsteps of that most quintessential of New York experiences: moving to the city, looking for an apartment, falling in love with the frenetic tempo around us. Charles Dickens, Louisa May Alcott and

Jacob Riis shed light on the city's nineteenth-century contradictions and struggle for a more equitable city. A variety of poets – among them, Walt Whitman and Emma Lazarus, Claude McKay and Langston Hughes, Elizabeth Bishop and Allen Ginsberg – offer an evocative taste of not just the poetry of the city but the poetry with which the city itself came to be most identified. Dawn Powell gives us a glimpse of New York on the cusp of war, while Jess Row depicts the many forms of grief that followed 9/11. Margaret Fuller captures the social and intellectual possibility she found in New York, while Djuna Barnes and Helen Keller render the magic of the city through its rich sensory symphony of smells, tastes and sounds. Together, they welcome us to find out just who we might become if we make this city our own.

NEW YORK

A Literary Anthology

OLD NEW YORK, LOST NEW YORK

WASHINGTON IRVING
(1783–1859)

Washington Irving was America's first transatlantic literary celebrity, and is often hailed as its first great man of letters. But his other claim to fame is that he was the first major American writer to be born and raised in New York City and helped to put that city on the world's literary map. Irving got his start by writing satirical sketches for a local New York newspaper in his teens, but was forced to divide his time between his writing and various lacklustre careers in law and business to pay the bills. The bankruptcy of his family's business emboldened him to launch his literary career in his thirties with the publication of *The Sketch Book* (1820), an enormously popular collection of essays and stories which included some of his still best-known works, among them 'Rip Van Winkle' and 'The Legend of Sleepy Hollow'. In this extract, drawn from Irving's satirical 1809 *Knickerbocker's History of New York*, the putative narrator – Diedrich Knickerbocker, a pedantic Dutch-American historian – tells us his version of how Manhattan came to be so named.

from Knickerbocker's History of New York

CONTAINING AN ATTEMPT AT ETYMOLOGY—AND OF THE FOUNDING OF THE GREAT CITY OF NEW AMSTERDAM

The original name of the island, whereon the squadron of Communipaw was thus propitiously thrown, is a matter of some dispute, and has already undergone considerable vitiation,—a melancholy proof of the instability of all sublunary things, and the vanity of all our hopes of lasting fame; for who can expect his name will live to posterity, when even the names of mighty islands are thus soon lost in contradiction and uncertainty!

The name most current at the present day, and which is likewise countenanced by the great historian Vander Donck, is MANHATTAN; which is said to have originated in a custom among the squaws, in the early settlement, of wearing men's hats, as is still done among many tribes. "Hence," as we are told by an old governor who was somewhat of a wag, and flourished almost a century since, and had paid a visit to the wits of Philadelphia,—"hence arose the appellation of man-hat-on, first given to the Indians, and afterwards to the island,"—a stupid joke! but well enough for a governor.

Among the more venerable sources of information on this subject is that valuable history of the American possessions, written by Master Richard Blome, in 1687, wherein it is called Manhadaes and Manahanent; nor must I forget the excellent little book, full of precious matter, of that authentic historian John Josselyn, Gent., who expressly calls it Manadaes.

Another etymology, still more ancient, and sanctioned by the countenance of our ever-to-be-lamented Dutch ancestors, is that found in certain letters still extant, which passed between the early governors and their neighboring powers, wherein it is called indifferently Monhattoes, Munhatos, and Manhattoes, which are evidently unimportant variations of the same name; for our wise forefathers set little store by those niceties either in orthography or orthoepy, which form the sole study and ambition of many learned men and women of this hypercritical age. This last name is said to be derived from the great Indian spirit Manetho, who was supposed to make this island his favorite abode, on account of its uncommon delights. For the Indian traditions affirm that the bay was once a translucid lake, filled with silver and golden fish, in the midst of which lay this beautiful island, covered with every variety of fruits and flowers; but that the sudden irruption of the Hudson laid waste these blissful scenes, and Manetho took his flight beyond the great waters of Ontario.

These, however, are very fabulous legends, to which very cautious credence must be given; and though I am willing to admit the last-quoted orthography of the name as very fit for prose, yet is there another which I peculiarly delight in, as at once poetical, melodious, and significant, and which we have on the authority of Master Juet, who, in his account of the voyage of the great Hudson, calls this MANNA-HATA, that is to say, the island of manna, or, in other words, a land flowing with milk and honey.

Still, my deference to the learned obliges me to notice the opinion of the worthy Dominie Heckwelder, which ascribes the name to a great drunken bout held on the island by the Dutch discoverers, whereat they made certain of the natives most ecstatically drunk for the first time in their lives; who, being delighted with their jovial entertainment, gave the place the name of Mannahattanink, that is to say, The Island of Jolly Topers: a name which it continues to merit to the present day.

HENRY JAMES
(1843–1916)

Henry James is best known for being a pre-eminent expatriate writer who penned some of the masterworks of nineteenth-century American fiction during the nearly four decades he spent living abroad in England. Many of his most famous novels – including *The Portrait of a Lady* (1881), *What Maisie Knew* (1897), *The Ambassadors* (1903) and *The Golden Bowl* (1904) – are set in Europe and turned an acute eye on what Americans and Europeans most miscalculate about each other. But he was a born New Yorker, and both his affection for his natal city and his ambivalence about the changes it underwent during his lifetime made their way into his fiction and essays. This delightful extract, drawn from his 1880 novel *Washington Square*, looks back on a moment relatively not long past in the city's history, when the environs around that eponymous square were still remarkably pastoral.

from Washington Square

Some three or four years before this, Doctor Sloper had moved his household gods up town, as they say in New York. He had been living ever since his marriage in an edifice of red brick, with granite copings and an enormous fan-light over the door, standing in a street within five minutes' walk of the City Hall, which saw its best days (from the social point of view) about 1820. After this, the tide of fashion began to set steadily northward, as, indeed, in New York, thanks to the narrow channel in which it flows, it is obliged to do, and the great hum of traffic rolled farther to the right and left of Broadway. By the time the Doctor changed his residence, the murmur of trade had become a mighty uproar, which was music in the ears of all good citizens interested in the commercial development, as they delighted to call it, of their fortunate isle. Doctor Sloper's interest in this phenomenon was only indirect—though, seeing that, as the years went on, half his patients came to be overworked men of business, it might have been more immediate—and when most of his neighbors' dwellings (also ornamented with granite copings and large fanlights) had been converted into offices, warehouses, and shipping agencies, and otherwise applied to the base uses of commerce, he determined to look out for a quieter home. The ideal of quiet and of genteel retirement, in 1835, was found in Washington Square, where the

Doctor built himself a handsome, modern, wide-fronted house, with a big balcony before the drawing-room windows, and a flight of white marble steps ascending to a portal which was also faced with white marble. This structure, and many of its neighbors, which it exactly resembled, were supposed, forty years ago, to embody the last results of architectural science, and they remain to this day very solid and honorable dwellings. In front of them was the square, containing a considerable quantity of inexpensive vegetation, enclosed by a wooden paling, which increased its rural and accessible appearance; and round the corner was the more august precinct of the Fifth Avenue, taking its origin at this point with a spacious and confident air which already marked it for high destinies. I know not whether it is owing to the tenderness of early associations, but this portion of New York appears to many persons the most delectable. It has a kind of established repose which is not of frequent occurrence in other quarters of the long, shrill city; it has a riper, richer, more honorable look than any of the upper ramifications of the great longitudinal thoroughfare—the look of having had something of a social history. It was here, as you might have been informed on good authority, that you had come into a world which appeared to offer a variety of sources of interest; it was here that your grandmother lived, in venerable solitude, and dispensed a hospitality which commended itself alike to the infant imagination and the infant palate; it was here that you took your first walks abroad, following the nursery-maid with unequal step, and sniffing up the strange odor of the ailanthus-trees which at that time formed the principal umbrage of the Square, and diffused an aroma that you were not yet critical enough to dislike as it deserved; it was here, finally, that your first school, kept by a broad-bosomed, broad-based old lady with a ferule, who was always having tea in a blue cup, with a saucer that didn't match, enlarged the circle both of your observations and your sensations. It was here, at any rate, that my heroine spent many years of her life; which is my excuse for this topographical parenthesis.

Mrs. Almond lived much farther up town, in an embryonic street, with a high number—a region where the extension of the city began to assume a theoretic air, where poplars grew beside the pavement (when there was one), and mingled their shade with the steep roofs of desultory Dutch houses, and where pigs and chickens disported themselves in the gutter. These elements of rural picturesqueness have now wholly departed from New York street scenery; but they were to be found within the memory of middle-aged persons in quarters which now would blush to be reminded of them.

Lydia Maria Child
(1802–1880)

Lydia Maria Child was an enormously influential and prolific American writer in her day, renowned as a path-breaking editor, novelist, poet, children's writer and political crusader. Many of her most widely read works – including her first novel, *Hobomok* (1824), and her household manual, *The Frugal Housewife* (1829) – reflected her life in New England and her interest in rethinking its history. She moved to New York City in 1841 to take up the editorship of the prominent anti-slavery newspaper the *National Anti-Slavery Standard*, and the city dispatches she wrote for that paper gained a wide enough readership to merit their own volume, published four years later as *Letters from New-York*. As ever, Child brought her reformist eye to the crushing poverty and everyday brutalities that she witnessed on the streets of New York, but also an intense interest in capturing its many sides and under-appreciated beauty. In this letter, she confesses her great love for Battery Park.

from Letters from New-York

August 19, 1841.

You ask what is now my opinion of this great Babylon; and playfully remind me of former philippics, and a long string of vituperative alliterations, such as magnificence and mud, finery and filth, diamonds and dirt, bullion and brass-tape, &c. &c. Nor do you forget my first impression of the city, when we arrived at early dawn, amid fog and drizzling rain, the expiring lamps adding their smoke to the impure air, and close beside us a boat called the 'Fairy Queen,' laden with dead hogs.

Well, Babylon remains the same as then. The din of crowded life, and the eager chase for gain, still run through its streets, like the perpetual murmur of a hive. Wealth dozes on French couches, thrice piled, and canopied with damask, while Poverty camps on the dirty pavement, or sleeps off its wretchedness in the watchhouse. There, amid the splendour of Broadway, sits the blind negro beggar, with horny hand and tattered garments, while opposite to him stands the stately mansion of the slave trader, still plying his bloody trade, and laughing to scorn the cobweb laws, through which the strong can break so easily.

In Wall-street, and elsewhere, Mammon, as usual, coolly calculates his chance of extracting a penny from war, pestilence, and famine; and Commerce, with her loaded drays, and jaded skeletons of horses, is busy as ever fulfilling the 'World's contract with the Devil.' The noisy discord of the street-cries gives the ear no rest; and the weak voice of weary childhood often makes the heart ache for the poor little wanderer, prolonging his task far into the hours of night. Sometimes, the harsh sounds are pleasantly varied by some feminine voice, proclaiming in musical cadence, 'Hot corn! hot corn!' with the poetic addition of 'Lily white corn! Buy my lily white corn!' When this sweet, wandering voice salutes my ear, my heart replies—

'Tis a glancing gleam o' the gift of song—
And the soul that speaks hath suffered wrong.

There *was* a time when all these things would have passed by me like the flitting figures of the magic lantern, or the changing scenery of a theatre, sufficient for the amusement of an hour. But now, I have lost the power of looking merely on the surface. Every thing seems to me to come from the Infinite, to be filled with the Infinite, to be tending toward the Infinite. Do I see crowds of men hastening to extinguish a fire? I see not merely uncouth garbs, and fantastic flickering lights of lurid hue, like a tramping troop of gnomes,—but straightway my mind is filled with thoughts about mutual helpfulness, human sympathy, the common bond of brotherhood, and the mysteriously deep foundations on which society rests; or rather, on which it now reels and totters.

But I am cutting the lines deep, when I meant only to give you an airy, unfinished sketch. I will answer your question, by saying, that though New-York remains the same, I like it better. This is partly because I am like the Lady's Delight, ever prone to take root, and look up with a smile, in whatever soil you place it; and partly because bloated disease, and black gutters, and pigs uglier than their ugly kind, no longer constitute the foreground in my picture of New-York. I have become more familiar with the pretty parks, dotted about here and there; with the shaded alcoves of the various public gardens; with blooming nooks, and 'sunny spots of greenery.' I am fast inclining to the belief, that the Battery rivals our beautiful Boston Common. The fine old trees are indeed wanting; but the newly-planted groves offer the light, flexile gracefulness of youth, to compete with their matured majesty of age. In extent, and variety of surface, this noble promenade is greatly inferior to ours; but there is

> The sea, the sea, the open sea;
> The fresh, the bright, the ever free.

Most fitting symbol of the Infinite, this trackless pathway of a world! heaving and stretching to meet the sky it never reaches—like the eager, unsatisfied aspirations of the human soul. The most beautiful landscape is imperfect without this feature. In the eloquent language of Lamartine—'The sea is to the scenes of nature what the eye is to a fine countenance; it illuminates them, it imparts to them that radiant physiognomy, which makes them live, speak, enchant, and fascinate the attention of those who contemplate them.'

If you deem me heretical in preferring the Battery to the Common, consecrated by so many pleasant associations of my youth, I know you will forgive me, if you will go there in the silence of midnight, to meet the breeze on your cheek, like the kiss of a friend; to hear the continual plashing of the sea, like the cool sound of oriental fountains; to see the moon look lovingly on the sea-nymphs, and throw down wealth of jewels on their shining hair; to look on the ships in their dim and distant beauty, each containing within itself, a little world of human thought, and human passion. Or go, when 'night, with her thousand eyes, looks down into the heart, making it also great'—when she floats above us, dark and solemn, and scarcely sees her image in the black mirror of the ocean. The city lamps surround you, like a shining belt of descended constellations, fit for the zone of Urania; while the pure bright stars peep through the dancing foliage, and speak to the soul of thoughtful shepherds on the ancient plains of Chaldea. And there, like mimic Fancy, playing fantastic freaks in the very presence of heavenly Imagination, stands Castle Garden—with its gay perspective of coloured lamps, like a fairy grotto, where imprisoned fire-spirits send up sparkling wreaths, or rockets laden with glittering ear-drops, caught by the floating sea-nymphs, as they fall.

But if you would see the Battery in *all* its glory, look at it when, through the misty mantle of retreating dawn, is seen the golden light of the rising sun! Look at the horizon, where earth, sea, and sky, kiss each other, in robes of reflected glory! The ships stretch their sails to the coming breeze, and glide majestically along—fit and graceful emblems of the Past; steered by Necessity; the Will constrained by outward Force. Quick as a flash, the steamboat passes them by—its rapidly revolving wheel made golden by the sunlight, and dropping diamonds to the laughing Nereides, profusely as pearls from Prince Esterhazy's embroidered coat. In that steamer, see you not an appropriate type of the busy, powerful, self-conscious Present? Of man's Will conquering outward Force; and thus making the elements his servants?

JAMES D. McCABE
(1842–1882)

James D. McCabe was a prolific Southern writer who published more than thirty biographies, histories and collections of poetry during his lifetime. But his most widely read works, originally published under the pseudonym Edward Martin, were a tremendously popular series of books devoted to dishing up the sunniest and seediest sides of nineteenth-century New York, including *The Secrets of the Great City* (1868), *Lights and Shadows of New York Life* (1872) and *New York by Sunlight and Gaslight* (1882). Written for middle-class readers keen to learn more about urban life in one of America's most rapidly expanding cities, McCabe's sketches were modelled on Charles Dickens's sketches of London in *Sketches by Boz* (1836) and Eugène Sue's 1843 novel *Les Mystères de Paris*, and intermingled titillating revelations and captivating urban haunts. In this extract, he praises the liberality of the New York mindset, laments its already skyrocketing rental prices and unfurls some of the now largely forgotten holiday traditions unique to the city.

from The Secrets of the Great City

Strangers coming to New York are struck with the fact that there are but two classes in the city—the poor and the rich. The middle class, which is so numerous in other cities, hardly exists at all here. The reason of this is plain to the initiated. Living in New York is so expensive that persons of moderate means reside in the suburbs, some of them as far as forty miles in the country. They come into the city, to their business, in crowds, between the hours of seven and nine in the morning, and literally pour out of it between four and seven in the evening. In fair weather the inconvenience of such a life is trifling, but in the winter it is absolutely fearful. A deep snow will sometimes obstruct the railroad tracks, and persons living outside of the city are either unable to leave New York, or are forced to spend the night on the cars. Again, the rivers will be so full of floating ice as to render it very dangerous, if not impossible, for the ferry boats to cross. At such times the railroad depots and ferry houses are crowded with persons anxiously awaiting transportation to their homes. The detention in New York, however, is not the greatest inconvenince caused by such mishaps. Many persons are frequently unable to reach the city, and thus lose several days from their business, at times when they can ill afford it.

We have already referred to the scarcity of houses.

The population of the city increases so rapidly that house-room cannot be provided for all. House rent is very high in New York. A house for a family of six persons, in a moderately respectable neighborhood, will rent for from sixteen hundred to twenty-five hundred dollars, the rate increasing as the neighborhood improves. On the fashionable streets, houses rent for from six thousand to fifteen thousand dollars per annum. These, it must be remembered, are palatial. Many persons owning these houses, live in Europe, or in other parts of the country, and pay all their expenses with the rent thus secured.

In consequence of this scarcity of dwellings, and the enormous rents asked for them, few families have residences of their own. People of moderate means generally rent a house, and sub-let a part of it to another family, take boarders, or rent furnished or unfurnished rooms to lodgers.

Furniture is expensive, and many persons prefer to rent furnished houses. These are always in demand, and in good localities command enormous prices. Heavy security has to be given by the lessee in such cases, as, without this, the tenant might make away with the furniture. Many persons owning houses for rent, furnish them at their own expense, and let them, the heavy rent soon paying a handsome profit on the furniture.

Persons living in a rented house are constantly apprehensive. Except in cases of long leases, no one knows how much his rent may be increased the next year. This causes a constant shifting of quarters, and is expensive and vexatious in the highest degree. It is partly due to the unsettled condition of the currency, but mainly to the scarcity of houses.

Many—indeed, the majority of the better class of inhabitants—prefer to board. Hotels and boarding houses pay well in New York. They are always full, and their prosperity has given rise to the remark that, "New York is a vast boarding house." We shall discuss this portion of our subject more fully in another chapter.

To persons of means, New York offers more advantages as a place of residence than any city in the land. Its delightful climate, its cosmopolitan and metropolitan character, and the endless variety of its attractions, render it the most delightful home in America. That this is true is shown by the fact that few persons who have lived in New York for twelve months ever care to leave it. Even those who could do better elsewhere are powerless to resist its fascinations.

THE HOLIDAYS IN THE CITY.

New York is very careful to observe the holidays, of the year. The mixture of the old Dutch, the orthodox English, and the Puritan elements has tended to preserve, in all its purity, each of the festivals which were so dear to our fathers. The New Yorker celebrates his Thanksgiving with all the fervor of a New Englander, and at the same time keeps his Christmas feast as heartily as his forefathers did, while the New Year is honored by a special observance.

NEW YEAR'S DAY.

New Year's day is one of the institutions of New York. Its observance was instituted by the Dutch, who made it a point never to enter upon the new season with any but the most cheerful spirits. They made it a time for renewing old friendships, and for wishing each other well. Each family was then sure to be at home, and social mirth and enjoyment ruled the hour. Old feuds were forgotten, family breaches were healed, and no one thought of harboring any but kindly feelings for his relatives or friends. The jolly old Knickerbocker sat in the warm light of his huge hearth, and smoked his long pipe in happiness and peace, while his children and children's children made merry round about him.

Subsequent generations have continued to observe the custom, and to-day it is as vigorous and fresh as it was when New Amsterdam was in its primitive glory.

GETTING READY.

For weeks before the New Year dawns, nearly every house in the city is in a state of confusion. The whole establishment is thoroughly overhauled and cleaned, and neither mistress nor maid have any rest from their labors. The men folks are nuisances at such times, and gradually keep themselves out of the way, lest they should interfere with the cleaning. Persons who contemplate refurnishing their houses, generally wait until near the close of the year before doing so, in order that everything may be new on the great day. Those who cannot refurnish, endeavor to make their establishments look as fresh and new as possible. A general baking, brewing, stewing, broiling, and frying is begun, and the pantries are loaded with good things to eat and to drink.

All the family must have new outfits for the occasion, and tailors and *modistes* find this a profitable season. To be seen in a dress that has ever been worn before, is considered the height of vulgarity.

The table is set in magnificent style. Elegant china and glassware, and splendid plate, adorn it. It is loaded down with dainties of every description. Wines, lemonades, coffee, brandy, whiskey and punch are in abundance. Punch is seen in all its glory on this day, and each householder strives to have the best of this article. There are regular punch-makers in the city, who reap a harvest at this time. Their services are engaged long beforehand, and they are kept busy all the morning going from house to house, to make this beverage which is nowhere so palatable as in this city.

Hairdressers, or "artistes in hair," as they call themselves, are also in demand at New Year, for each lady then wishes to have her *coiffure* as magnificent as possible. This is a day of hard work to these *artistes,* and in order to meet all their engagements, they begin their rounds at midnight. They are punctual to the moment, and from that time until noon on New Year's day are busily engaged. Of course those whose heads are dressed at such unseasonable hours cannot think of lying down to sleep, as their "head gear" would be ruined by such a procedure. They are compelled to rest sitting bolt upright, or with their heads resting on a table or the back of a chair.

Sometimes a family desiring to "shine" on such occasions find themselves unable, after meeting the other expenses, to provide the clothing and jewels necessary. These are then hired from *modistes* and jewelers, proper security being given for their return.

NEW YEAR'S CALLS.

All New York is stirring by eight o'clock. By nine, the streets are filled with gayly dressed persons on their way to make their annual calls. Private carriages, hacks and other vehicles soon appear, filled with persons bent upon similar expeditions. Business is entirely suspended in the city, the day is a legal holiday, and is faithfully observed by all classes. Hack hire is enormous—forty or fifty dollars being the price of a carriage for the day. The cars are crowded, and, if the weather is fine, everybody is in the highest spirits. A stranger is struck with the fact that the crowd in the streets consists almost entirely of men. Women rarely venture out on this day. It is not considered respectable, and, the truth is, it is not safe to do so.

The earliest hour at which a call can be paid, is ten o'clock. The ultra fashionables do not begin to "receive" until twelve. At the proper time, the lady of the house, attended by her daughters, if she has any, takes her stand in the drawing room by the hospitable board. In a little while, the door bell rings, and the first visitor is introduced. He salutes his hostess, and after a few pleasant words, is invited to partake of the refreshments. A few eatables are swallowed in haste—the visitor talking away all the while with his mouth full—a glass of wine or of punch is "gulped" down, and the gentleman bows himself out. He has no time to lose, for he has dozens of similar calls to make. This goes on until late at night.

A gentleman in starting out, provides himself with a written list of the calls he intends making, and "checks" each one off with his pencil, when made. This list is necessary, as few sober men can remember all their friends on such occasions, and after the first dozen visits are over, such a list is greatly needed. Each man tries to make as many calls as possible, so that he may boast of the feat afterwards. At the outset, of course, everything is conducted with the utmost propriety, but, as the day wears on, the generous liquors they have imbibed begin to "tell" upon the callers, and many cocentricities to use no harsher term, are the result. Towards the close of the day, everything is in confusion—the door bell is never silent. Crowds of young men in various stages of intoxication rush into the lighted parlors, leer at the hostess in the vain effort to offer their respects, call for liquor, drink it, and stagger out, to repeat the scene at some other house. Frequently, they are unable to recognize the residences of their friends, and stagger into the wrong house. Some fall early in the day, and are put to bed by their friends; others sink down helpless at the feet of their hostess, and are sent home; and a few manage to get through the day. Strange as it may seem, it is no disgrace to get drunk on New Year's day. These indiscretions are expected at such times; and it not unfrequently happens that the ladies, themselves, succumb to the seductive influences of "punch" towards the close of the evening, and are put to bed by the servants. Those who do retire sober, are thoroughly worn out.

THE NEXT DAY.

The next day one half of New York is sick. Doctors are in demand. Headaches and various other ailments caused by "punch" are frequent. Business men have a weary, sleepless look, and it requires one or two nights' rest to restore mind and body to their proper condition. Should you call on a lady friend, you will probably find her indisposed—the cause of her sickness you can easily imagine. The Police Courts are busy on the Second of January. Disorder, drunkenness, and fighting are frequent on New Year's night.

INDEPENDENCE DAY.

The Fourth of July is simply a nuisance in New York. The weather is generally very warm. There is an early parade of the First Division of the National Guard, and at night there are fine displays of fireworks in various parts of the city. The greater part of the day, however, is devoted to drinking and acts of lawlessness.

Fire-crackers, Roman candles, pin-wheels, and the like, abound. The police try to stop them, but without success. The city resounds with the discharges, the air is filled with sulphurous vapors, which irritate the throat and eyes, and the ears are stunned with the explosions. Young America is in his glory, and quiet, orderly people are driven nearly frantic.

EDITH WHARTON
(1862–1937)

Although she would spend the final three decades of her life as an expatriate American writer in Paris, and took inspiration throughout her life from her many travels through Europe, Edith Wharton was born in New York City – and both New York and the upper-class life into which she was born continued to captivate her attention throughout her career. In novels such as *The House of Mirth* (1905), *The Custom of the Country* (1913) and *The Age of Innocence* (1920), she brought an acutely attentive eye to the sumptuous interiors and stifling boredom that marked so much of upper-crust life in the city. This in turn garnered her acclaim (and a Pulitzer Prize) in her own day and continuing interest from readers and film-makers in ours. In this short story, first published in *Scribner's Magazine* in 1891, Wharton offers readers an evocative glimpse of a surprisingly different slice of Old New York through the eyes of an ageing widow taking in the city's day-to-day noise and fast-disappearing greenery through her boarding-house window.

Mrs. Manstey's View

The view from Mrs. Manstey's window was not a striking one, but to her at least it was full of interest and beauty. Mrs. Manstey occupied the back room on the third floor of a New York boarding-house, in a street where the ash-barrels lingered late on the sidewalk and the gaps in the pavement would have staggered a Quintus Curtius. She was the widow of a clerk in a large wholesale house, and his death had left her alone, for her only daughter had married in California, and could not afford the long journey to New York to see her mother. Mrs. Manstey, perhaps, might have joined her daughter in the West, but they had now been so many years apart that they had ceased to feel any need of each other's society, and their intercourse had long been limited to the exchange of a few perfunctory letters, written with indifference by the daughter, and with difficulty by Mrs. Manstey, whose right hand was growing stiff with gout. Even had she felt a stronger desire for her daughter's companionship, Mrs. Manstey's increasing infirmity, which caused her to dread the three flights of stairs between her room and the street, would have given her pause on the eve of undertaking so long a journey; and without, perhaps, formulating these reasons she had long since accepted as a matter of course her solitary life in New York.

She was, indeed, not quite lonely, for a few friends

still toiled up now and then to her room; but their visits grew rare as the years went by. Mrs. Manstey had never been a sociable woman, and during her husband's lifetime his companionship had been all-sufficient to her. For many years she had cherished a desire to live in the country, to have a hen-house and a garden; but this longing had faded with age, leaving only in the breast of the uncommunicative old woman a vague tenderness for plants and animals. It was, perhaps, this tenderness which made her cling so fervently to the view from her window, a view in which the most optimistic eye would at first have failed to discover anything admirable.

Mrs. Manstey, from her coign of vantage (a slightly projecting bow-window where she nursed an ivy and a succession of unwholesome-looking bulbs), looked out first upon the yard of her own dwelling, of which, however, she could get but a restricted glimpse. Still, her gaze took in the topmost boughs of the ailanthus below her window, and she knew how early each year the clump of dicentra strung its bending stalk with hearts of pink.

But of greater interest were the yards beyond. Being for the most part attached to boarding-houses they were in a state of chronic untidiness and fluttering, on certain days of the week, with miscellaneous garments and frayed table-cloths. In spite of this Mrs. Manstey found much to admire in the long vista which she commanded. Some of the yards were, indeed, but stony wastes, with grass in the cracks of the pavement and no shade in spring save that afforded by the intermittent leafage of the clothes-lines. These yards Mrs. Manstey disapproved of, but the others, the green ones, she loved. She had grown used to their disorder; the broken barrels, the empty bottles and paths unswept no longer annoyed her; hers was the happy faculty of dwelling on the pleasanter side of the prospect before her.

In the very next enclosure did not a magnolia open its hard white flowers against the watery blue of April? And was there not, a little way down the line, a fence foamed over every May by lilac waves of wistaria? Farther still, a horse-chestnut lifted its candelabra of buff and pink blossoms above broad fans of foliage; while in the opposite yard June was sweet with the breath of a neglected syringa, which persisted in growing in spite of the countless obstacles opposed to its welfare.

But if nature occupied the front rank in Mrs. Manstey's view, there was much of a more personal character to interest her in the aspect of the houses and their inmates. She deeply disapproved of the mustard-colored curtains which had lately been hung in the doctor's window opposite; but she glowed with pleasure when the house farther down had its old bricks washed with a coat of paint. The occupants of the houses did not often show themselves at the back windows, but the servants were always in sight. Noisy slatterns, Mrs. Manstey pronounced the greater number; she knew their ways and hated them. But to the quiet cook in the newly painted house, whose mistress bullied her, and who secretly fed the stray cats at nightfall, Mrs. Manstey's warmest sympathies were given. On one occasion her feelings were racked by the neglect of a housemaid, who for two days forgot to feed the parrot committed to her care. On the third day, Mrs. Manstey, in spite of her gouty hand, had just penned a letter, beginning: "Madam, it is now three days since your parrot has been fed," when the forgetful maid appeared at the window with a cup of seed in her hand.

But in Mrs. Manstey's more meditative moods it was the narrowing perspective of far-off yards which pleased her best. She loved, at twilight, when the distant brownstone spire seemed melting in the fluid yellow of the west, to lose herself in vague memories of a trip to Europe, made years ago, and now reduced in her mind's eye to a pale phantasmagoria of indistinct steeples and dreamy skies. Perhaps at heart Mrs. Manstey was an artist; at all events she was sensible of many changes of color unnoticed by the average eye, and dear to her as the green of early spring was the black lattice of branches against a cold sulphur sky at the close of a snowy day. She enjoyed, also, the sunny thaws of March, when patches of earth showed through the snow, like ink-spots spreading on a sheet of white blotting-paper; and, better still, the haze of boughs, leafless but swollen, which replaced the clear-cut tracery of winter. She even watched with a certain interest the trail of smoke from a far-off factory chimney, and missed a detail in the landscape when the factory was closed and the smoke disappeared.

Mrs. Manstey, in the long hours which she spent at

her window, was not idle. She read a little, and knitted numberless stockings; but the view surrounded and shaped her life as the sea does a lonely island. When her rare callers came it was difficult for her to detach herself from the contemplation of the opposite window-washing, or the scrutiny of certain green points in a neighboring flowerbed which might, or might not, turn into hyacinths, while she feigned an interest in her visitor's anecdotes about some unknown grandchild. Mrs. Manstey's real friends were the denizens of the yards, the hyacinths, the magnolia, the green parrot, the maid who fed the cats, the doctor who studied late behind his mustard-colored curtains; and the confidant of her tenderer musings was the church-spire floating in the sunset.

One April day, as she sat in her usual place, with knitting cast aside and eyes fixed on the blue sky mottled with round clouds, a knock at the door announced the entrance of her landlady. Mrs. Manstey did not care for her landlady, but she submitted to her visits with ladylike resignation. To-day, however, it seemed harder than usual to turn from the blue sky and the blossoming magnolia to Mrs. Sampson's unsuggestive face, and Mrs. Manstey was conscious of a distinct effort as she did so.

"The magnolia is out earlier than usual this year, Mrs. Sampson," she remarked, yielding to a rare impulse, for she seldom alluded to the absorbing interest of her life. In the first place it was a topic not likely to appeal to her visitors and, besides, she lacked the power of expression and could not have given utterance to her feelings had she wished to.

"The what, Mrs. Manstey?" inquired the landlady, glancing about the room as if to find there the explanation of Mrs. Manstey's statement.

"The magnolia in the next yard—in Mrs. Black's yard," Mrs. Manstey repeated.

"Is it, indeed? I didn't know there was a magnolia there," said Mrs. Sampson, carelessly. Mrs. Manstey looked at her; she did not know that there was a magnolia in the next yard!

"By the way," Mrs. Sampson continued, "speaking of Mrs. Black reminds me that the work on the extension is to begin next week.

"The what?" it was Mrs. Manstey's turn to ask.

"The extension," said Mrs. Sampson, nodding her head in the direction of the ignored magnolia. "You knew, of course, that Mrs. Black was going to build an extension to her house? Yes, ma'am, I hear it is to run right back to the end of the yard. How she can afford to build an extension in these hard times I don't see; but she always was crazy about building. She used to keep a boarding-house in Seventeeth Street, and she nearly ruined herself then by sticking out bow-windows and what not; I should have thought that would have cured her of building, but I guess it's a disease, like drink. Anyhow, the work is to begin on Monday."

Mrs. Manstey had grown pale. She always spoke slowly, so the landlady did not heed the long pause which followed. At last Mrs. Manstey said: "Do you know how high the extension will be?"

"That's the most absurd part of it. The extension is to be built right up to the roof of the main building: now, did you ever?"

Mrs. Manstey paused again. "Won't it be a great annoyance to you, Mrs. Sampson?" she asked.

"I should say it would. But there's no help for it; if people have got a mind to build extensions there's no law to prevent 'em, that I'm aware of." Mrs. Manstey, knowing this, was silent. "There is no help for it." Mrs. Sampson repeated, "but if I *am* a church member, I wouldn't be so sorry if it ruined Eliza Black. Well, good-day, Mrs. Manstey; I'm glad to find you so comfortable."

So comfortable—so comfortable! Left to herself the old woman turned once more to the window. How lovely the view was that day! The blue sky with its round clouds shed a brightness over everything; the ailanthus had put on a tinge of yellow-green, the hyacinths were budding, the magnolia flowers looked more than ever like rosettes carved in alabaster. Soon the wistaria would bloom, then the horse-chestnut; but not for her. Between her eyes and them a barrier of brick and mortar would swiftly rise; presently even the spire would disappear, and all her radiant world be blotted out. Mrs. Manstey sent away untouched the dinner-tray brought to her that evening. She lingered in the window until the windy sunset died in bat-colored dusk; then, going to bed, she lay sleepless all night.

Early the next day she was up and at the window. It was raining, but even through the slanting gray gauze the scene had its charm—and then the rain was so good for the trees. She had noticed the day before that the ailanthus was growing dusty.

"Of course I might move," said Mrs. Manstey aloud, and turning from the window she looked about her room. She might move, of course; so might she be flayed alive; but she was not likely to survive either operation. The room, though far less important to her happiness than the view, was as much a part of her existence. She had lived in it seventeen years. She knew every stain on the wallpaper, every rent in the carpet; the light fell in a certain way on her engravings, her books had grown shabby on their shelves, her bulbs and ivy were used to their window and knew which way to lean to the sun. "We are all too old to move," she said.

That afternoon it cleared. Wet and radiant the blue reappeared through torn rags of cloud; the ailanthus sparkled; the earth in the flower-borders looked rich and warm. It was Thursday, and on Monday the building of the extension was to begin.

On Sunday afternoon a card was brought to Mrs. Black, as she was engaged in gathering up the fragments of the boarders' dinner in the basement. The card, black-edged, bore Mrs. Manstey's name.

"One of Mrs. Sampson's boarders; wants to move, I suppose. Well, I can give her a room next year in the extension. Dinah," said Mrs. Black, "tell the lady I'll be upstairs in a minute."

Mrs. Black found Mrs. Manstey standing in the long parlor garnished with statuettes and antimacassars; in that house she could not sit down.

Stooping hurriedly to open the register, which let out a cloud of dust, Mrs. Black advanced to her visitor.

"I'm happy to meet you, Mrs. Manstey; take a seat, please," the landlady remarked in her prosperous voice, the voice of a woman who can afford to build extensions. There was no help for it; Mrs. Manstey sat down.

"Is there anything I can do for you, ma'am?" Mrs. Black continued. "My house is full at present, but I am going to build an extension, and——"

"It is about the extension that I wish to speak," said Mrs. Manstey, suddenly. "I am a poor woman, Mrs. Black, and I have never been a happy one. I shall have to talk about myself first to—to make you understand."

Mrs. Black, astonished but imperturbable, bowed at this parenthesis.

"I never had what I wanted," Mrs. Manstey continued. "It was always one disappointment after another. For years I wanted to live in the country. I dreamed and dreamed about it; but we never could manage it. There was no sunny window in our house, and so all my plants died. My daughter married years ago and went away—besides, she never cared for the same things. Then my husband died and I was left alone. That was seventeen years ago. I went to live at Mrs. Sampson's, and I have been there ever since. I have grown a little infirm, as you see, and I don't get out often; only on fine days, if I am feeling very well. So you can understand my sitting a great deal in my window—the back window on the third floor——"

"Well, Mrs. Manstey," said Mrs. Black, liberally, "I could give you a back room, I dare say; one of the new rooms in the ex——"

"But I don't want to move; I can't move," said Mrs. Manstey, almost with a scream. "And I came to tell you that if you build that extension I shall have no view from my window—no view! Do you understand?"

Mrs. Black thought herself face to face with a lunatic, and she had always heard that lunatics must be humored.

"Dear me, dear me," she remarked, pushing her chair back a little way, "that is too bad, isn't it? Why, I never thought of that. To be sure, the extension *will* interfere with your view, Mrs. Manstey."

"You do understand?" Mrs. Manstey gasped.

"Of course I do. And I'm real sorry about it, too. But there, don't you worry, Mrs. Manstey. I guess we can fix that all right."

Mrs. Manstey rose from her seat, and Mrs. Black slipped toward the door.

"What do you mean by fixing it? Do you mean that I can induce you to change your mind about the extension? Oh, Mrs. Black, listen to me. I have two thousand dollars in the bank and I could manage, I know I could manage, to give you a thousand if——" Mrs. Manstey paused; the tears were rolling down her cheeks.

"There, there, Mrs. Manstey, don't you worry," repeated Mrs. Black, soothingly. "I am sure we can settle it. I am sorry that I can't stay and talk about it any longer, but this is such a busy time of day, with supper to get——"

Her hand was on the door-knob, but with sudden vigor Mrs. Manstey seized her wrist

"You are not giving me a definite answer. Do you mean to say that you accept my proposition?"

"Why, I'll think it over, Mrs. Manstey, certainly I will. I wouldn't annoy you for the world—"

"But the work is to begin to-morrow, I am told," Mrs. Manstey persisted.

Mrs. Black hesitated. "It shan't begin, I promise you that; I'll send word to the builder this very night." Mrs. Manstey tightened her hold.

"You are not deceiving me, are you?" she said.

"No–no," stammered Mrs. Black. "How can you think such a thing of me, Mrs. Manstey?"

Slowly Mrs. Manstey's clutch relaxed, and she passed through the open door. "One thousand dollars," she repeated, pausing in the hall; then she let herself out of the house and hobbled down the steps, supporting herself on the cast-iron railing.

"My goodness," exclaimed Mrs. Black, shutting and bolting the hall-door, "I never knew the old woman was crazy! And she looks so quiet and ladylike, too."

Mrs. Manstey slept well that night, but early the next morning she was awakened by a sound of hammering. She got to her window with what haste she might and, looking out, saw that Mrs. Black's yard was full of workmen. Some were carrying loads of brick from the kitchen to the yard, others beginning to demolish the old-fashioned wooden balcony which adorned each story of Mrs. Black's house. Mrs. Manstey saw that she had been deceived. At first she thought of confiding her trouble to Mrs. Sampson, but a settled discouragement soon took possession of her and she went back to bed, not caring to see what was going on.

Toward afternoon, however, feeling that she must know the worst, she rose and dressed herself. It was a laborious task, for her hands were stiffer than usual, and the hooks and buttons seemed to evade her.

When she seated herself in the window, she saw that the workmen had removed the upper part of the balcony, and that the bricks had multiplied since morning. One of the men, a coarse fellow with a bloated face, picked a magnolia blossom and, after smelling it, threw it to the ground; the next man, carrying a load of bricks, trod on the flower in passing.

"Look out, Jim," called one of the men to another who was smoking a pipe, "if you throw matches around near those barrels of paper you'll have the old tinder-box burning down before you know it." And Mrs. Manstey, leaning forward, perceived that there were several barrels of paper and rubbish under the wooden balcony.

At length the work ceased and twilight fell. The sunset was perfect and a roseate light, transfiguring the distant spire, lingered late in the west. When it grew dark Mrs. Manstey drew down the shades and proceeded, in her usual methodical manner, to light her lamp. She always filled and lit it with her own hands, keeping a kettle of kerosene on a zinc-covered shelf in a closet. As the lamp-light filled the room it assumed its peaceful aspect. The books and pictures and plants seemed, like their mistress, to settle themselves down for another quiet evening, and Mrs. Manstey, as was her wont, drew up her armchair to the table and began to knit.

That night she could not sleep. The weather had changed and a wild wind was abroad, blotting the stars with close-driven clouds. Mrs. Manstey rose once or twice and looked out of the window; but of the view nothing was discernible save a tardy light or two in the opposite windows. These lights at last went out, and Mrs. Manstey, who had watched for their extinction, began to dress herself. She was in evident haste, for she merely flung a thin dressing-gown over her night-dress and wrapped her head in a scarf; then she opened her closet and cautiously took out the kettle of kerosene. Having slipped a bundle of wooden matches into her pocket she proceeded, with increasing precautions, to unlock her door, and a few moments later she was feeling her way down the dark staircase, led by a glimmer of gas from the lower hall. At length she reached the bottom of the stairs and began the more difficult descent into the utter darkness of the basement. Here, however, she could move more freely, as there was less danger of being overheard; and without much delay she contrived to unlock the iron door leading into the yard. A gust of cold wind smote her as she stepped out and groped shiveringly under the clothes-lines.

That morning at three o'clock an alarm of fire brought the engines to Mrs. Black's door, and also brought Mrs. Sampson's startled boarders to their windows. The wooden balcony at the back of Mrs. Black's house was ablaze, and among those who watched the progress of the flames was Mrs. Manstey, leaning in her thin dressing-gown from the open window.

The fire, however, was soon put out, and the frightened occupants of the house, who had fled in scant attire, reassembled at dawn to find that little mischief had been done beyond the cracking of window panes and smoking of ceilings. In fact, the chief sufferer by the fire was Mrs. Manstey, who was found in the morning gasping with pneumonia, a not unnatural result, as everyone remarked, of her having hung out of an open window at her age in a dressing-gown. It was easy to see that she was very ill, but no one had guessed how grave the doctor's verdict would be, and the faces gathered that evening about Mrs. Sampson's table were awe-struck and disturbed. Not that any of the boarders knew Mrs. Manstey well; she "kept to herself," as they said, and seemed to fancy herself too good for them; but then it is always disagreeable to have anyone dying in the house, and, as one lady observed to another: "It might just as well have been you or me, my dear."

But it was only Mrs. Manstey; and she was dying, as she had lived, lonely if not alone. The doctor had sent a trained nurse, and Mrs. Sampson, with muffled step, came in from time to time; but both, to Mrs. Manstey, seemed remote and unsubstantial as the figures in a dream. All day she said nothing; but when she was asked for her daughter's address she shook her head. At times the nurse noticed that she seemed to be listening attentively for some sound which did not come; then again she dozed.

The next morning at daylight she was very low. The nurse called Mrs. Sampson, and as the two bent over the old woman they saw her lips move.

"Lift me up—out of bed," she whispered.

They raised her in their arms, and with her stiff hand she pointed to the window.

"Oh, the window—she wants to sit in the window. She used to sit there all day," Mrs. Sampson explained. "It can do her no harm, I suppose?"

"Nothing matters now," said the nurse.

They carried Mrs. Manstey to the window and placed her in her chair. The dawn was abroad, a jubilant spring dawn; the spire had already caught a golden ray, though the magnolia and horse-chestnut still slumbered in shadow. In Mrs. Black's yard all was quiet. The charred timbers of the balcony lay where they had fallen. It was evident that since the fire the builders had not returned to their work. The magnolia had unfolded a few more sculptural flowers; the view was undisturbed.

It was hard for Mrs. Manstey to breathe. Each moment it grew more difficult. She tried to make them open the window, but they would not understand. If she could have tasted the air, sweet with the penetrating ailanthus savor, it would have eased her; but the view at least was there—the spire was golden now, the heavens had warmed from pearl to blue, day was alight from east to west, even the magnolia had caught the sun.

Mrs. Manstey's head fell back, and smiling she died.

That day the building of the extension was resumed.

YUNG WING
(1828–1912)

Pioneering Chinese American author, educational reformer and diplomat Yung Wing is perhaps now best remembered for being the first Chinese student to graduate from an American university (Yale) in 1854. Throughout his remarkable life in China and the United States, Wing encouraged closer diplomatic and educational ties between the two countries, investigated the working conditions of Chinese immigrants, advocated for greater democratic reforms in China and worked to counter the climate of increasing hostility against Chinese immigrants in the US, the country he chose to make his home for many decades. This brief extract from his widely read 1909 autobiography, *My Life in China and America*, reminisces on his first visit to New York in 1845 and highlights the bustling metropolis it had become by the turn of the twentieth century.

from My Life in China and America

From St. Helena we took a northwesterly course and struck the Gulf Stream, which, with the wind still fair and favorable, carried us to New York in a short time. We landed in New York on the 12th of April, 1847, after a passage of ninety-eight days of unprecedented fair weather. The New York of 1847 was altogether a different city from the New York of 1909. It was a city of only 250,000 or 300,000 inhabitants; now it is a metropolis rivaling London in population, wealth and commerce. The whole of Manhattan Island is turned into a city of skyscrapers, churches and palatial residences.

Little did I realize when in 1845 I wrote, while in the Morrison School, a composition on "An Imaginary Voyage to New York and up the Hudson," that I was to see New York in reality. This incident leads me to the reflection that sometimes our imagination foreshadows what lies uppermost in our minds and brings possibilities within the sphere of realities.

Paule Marshall
(1929–2019)

Influential African American novelist Paule Marshall was born in Brooklyn to working-class parents from Barbados, and her writings gave powerful voice to the experience of the Caribbean community in New York City and the challenges of navigating both identities. Her first and still most widely read novel, *Brown Girl, Brownstones*, was published in 1959 to great acclaim. But she wrote eight standout works over the course of her career, including *Soul Clap Hands and Sing* (1961), *The Chosen Place, the Timeless People* (1969), *Praisesong for the Widow* (1983) and *The Fisher King* (2001), for which she would garner a Guggenheim Fellowship and a Dos Passos Prize, among other accolades. This extract, drawn from the opening chapter of her debut novel, presents a vision of Old New York through the eyes of a ten-year-old West Indian girl envisioning the lingering ghosts of the past residents of her family's Brooklyn brownstone.

from Brown Girl, Brownstones

In the somnolent July afternoon the unbroken line of brownstone houses down the long Brooklyn street resembled an army massed at attention. They were all one uniform red-brown stone. All with high massive stone stoops and black iron-grille fences staving off the sun. All draped in ivy as though mourning. Their façades, indifferent to the summer's heat and passion, faced a park while their backs reared dark against the sky. They were only three or four stories tall—squat— yet they gave the impression of formidable height.

Glancing down the Brooklyn street you thought of those joined brownstones as one house reflected through a train of mirrors, with no walls between the houses but only vast rooms yawning endlessly one into the other. Yet, looking close, you saw that under the thick ivy each house had something distinctively its own. Some touch that was Gothic, Romanesque, baroque or Greek triumphed amid the Victorian clutter. Here, Ionic columns framed the windows while next door gargoyles scowled up at the sun. There, the cornices were hung with carved foliage while Gorgon heads decorated others. Many houses had bay windows or Gothic stonework; a few boasted turrets raised high above the other roofs. Yet they all shared the same brown monotony. All seemed doomed by the confusion in their design.

Behind those grim façades, in those high rooms, life soared and ebbed. Bodies crouched in the postures of love at night, children burst from the womb's thick shell, and death, when it was time, shuffled through the halls. First, there had been the Dutch-English and Scotch-Irish who had built the houses. There had been tea in the afternoon then and skirts rustling across the parquet floors and mild voices. For a long time it had been only the whites, each generation unraveling in a quiet skein of years behind the green shades.

But now in 1939 the last of them were discreetly dying behind those shades or selling the houses and moving away. And as they left, the West Indians slowly edged their way in. Like a dark sea nudging its way onto a white beach and staining the sand, they came. The West Indians, especially the Barbadians who had never owned anything perhaps but a few poor acres in a poor land, loved the houses with the same fierce idolatry as they had the land on their obscure islands. But, with their coming, there was no longer tea in the afternoon, and their odd speech clashed in the hushed rooms, while underneath the ivy the old houses remained as indifferent to them as to the whites, as aloof . . .

Her house was alive to Selina. She sat this summer afternoon on the upper landing on the top floor, listening to its shallow breathing—a ten-year-old girl with scuffed legs and a body as straggly as the clothes she wore. A haze of sunlight seeping down from the skylight through the dust and dimness of the hall caught her wide full mouth, the small but strong nose, the eyes set deep in the darkness of her face. They were not the eyes of a child. Something too old lurked in their centers. They were weighted, it seemed, with scenes of a long life. She might have been old once and now, miraculously, young again—but with the memory of that other life intact. She seemed to know the world down there in the dark hall and beyond for what it was. Yet knowing, she still longed to leave this safe, sunlit place at the top of the house for the challenge there.

Suddenly the child, Selina, leaped boldly to the edge of the step, her lean body quivering. At the moment she hurled herself forward, her hand reached back to grasp the bannister, and the contradiction of her movement flung her back on the step. She huddled there, rubbing her injured elbow and hating her cowardice. Slowly she raised her arm, thin and dark in the sun-haze, circled by two heavy silver bangles which had come from "home" and which every Barbadian-American girl wore from birth. Glaring down, she shook her fist, and the bangles sounded her defiance with a thin clangor. When her arm dropped, the house, stunned by the noise, ceased breathing and a pure silence fell.

She smiled, for this was the silence she loved. It came when the old white servant upstairs slept amid her soiled sheets, when her father read and napped in the sun parlor, her sister slept in their basement bedroom and the new tenant Suggie was out. Above all, it was a silence which came when the mother was at work.

She rose, her arms lifted in welcome, and quickly the white family who had lived here before, whom the old woman upstairs always spoke of, glided with pale footfalls up the stairs. Their white hands trailed the bannister; their mild voices implored her to give them a little life. And as they crowded around, fusing with her, she was no longer a dark girl alone and dreaming at the top of an old house, but one of them, invested with their beauty and gentility. She threw her head back until it trembled proudly on the stalk of her neck and, holding up her imaginary gown, she swept downstairs to the parlor floor.

At the bottom step she paused in the entrance hall, which was a room in itself with its carpet, wallpaper and hushed dimness. Opening off the hall was the parlor, full of ponderous furniture and potted ferns which the whites had left, with an aged and inviolate silence. (It was the museum of all the lives that had ever lived here.) The floor-to-ceiling mirror retained their faces as the silence did their voices.

ON MOVING TO NEW YORK

EMMA GOLDMAN
(1869–1941)

Emma Goldman immigrated to the US from Lithuania as a teenager, and went on to become perhaps America's most famous radical. An impassioned speaker, a pioneering editor and an indomitable anarchist activist, Goldman regularly lectured on the topics of educational reform, free love, birth control access and gay rights to large audiences across the US. In part because of the reach of her lectures and wide readership of *Mother Earth* magazine, the radical periodical she founded in New York in 1906 and edited for a decade, she garnered the dubious distinction of being labelled 'the most dangerous woman in America' by J. Edgar Hoover, and ultimately would be deported from the US in 1919 for her anti-draft agitation during the First World War. But New York, the city to which she had moved aged twenty and the place where she first made her way as an activist and editor, was the great love of her life. In this selection from the opening pages of her 1931 autobiography, *Living My Life*, Goldman recounts her arrival in the dazzling city that transformed her life.

from Living My Life

It was the 15th of August 1889, the day of my arrival in New York City. I was twenty years old. All that had happened in my life until that time was now left behind me, cast off like a worn-out garment. A new world was before me, strange and terrifying. But I had youth, good health, and a passionate ideal. Whatever the new held in store for me I was determined to meet unflinchingly.

How well I remember that day! It was a Sunday. The West Shore train, the cheapest, which was all I could afford, had brought me from Rochester, New York, reaching Weehawken at eight o'clock in the morning. Thence I came by ferry to New York City. I had no friends there, but I carried three addresses, one of a married aunt, one of a young medical student I had met in New Haven a year before, while working in a corset factory there, and one of the *Freiheit,* a German anarchist paper published by Johann Most.

My entire possessions consisted of five dollars and a small hand-bag. My sewing-machine, which was to help me to independence, I had checked as baggage. Ignorant of the distance from West Forty-second Street to the Bowery, where my aunt lived, and unaware of the enervating heat of a New York day in August, I started out on foot. How confusing and endless a large city seems to the new-comer, how cold and unfriendly!

After receiving many directions and misdirections

and making frequent stops at bewildering intersections, I landed in three hours at the photographic gallery of my aunt and uncle. Tired and hot, I did not at first notice the consternation of my relatives at my unexpected arrival. They asked me to make myself at home, gave me breakfast, and then plied me with questions. Why did I come to New York? Had I definitely broken with my husband? Did I have money? What did I intend to do? I was told that I could, of course, stay with them. "Where else could you go, a young woman alone in New York?" Certainly, but I would have to look for a job immediately. Business was bad, and the cost of living high.

I heard it all as if in a stupor. I was too exhausted from my wakeful night's journey, the long walk, and the heat of the sun, which was already pouring down fiercely. The voices of my relatives sounded distant, like the buzzing of flies, and they made me drowsy. With an effort I pulled myself together. I assured them I did not come to impose myself on them; a friend living on Henry Street was expecting me and would put me up. I had but one desire—to get out, away from the prattling, chilling voices. I left my bag and departed.

The friend I had invented in order to escape the "hospitality" of my relatives was only a slight acquaintance, a young anarchist by the name of A. Solotaroff, whom I had once heard lecture in New Haven. Now I started out to find him. After a long search I discovered the house, but the tenant had left. The janitor, at first very brusque, must have noticed my despair. He said he would look for the address that the family left when they moved. Presently he came back with the name of the street, but there was no number. What was I to do? How to find Solotaroff in the vast city? I decided to stop at every house, first on one side of the street, and then on the other. Up and down, six flights of stairs, I tramped, my head throbbing, my feet weary. The oppressive day was drawing to a close. At last, when I was about to give up the search, I discovered him on Montgomery Street, on the fifth floor of a tenement house seething with humanity.

A year had passed since our first meeting, but Solotaroff had not forgotten me. His greeting was genial and warm, as of an old friend. He told me that he shared his small apartment with his parents and little brother, but that I could have his room; he would stay with a fellow-student for a few nights. He assured me that I would have no difficulty in finding a place; in fact, he knew two sisters who were living with their father in a two-room flat. They were looking for another girl to join them. After my new friend had fed me tea and some delicious Jewish cake his mother had baked, he told me about the different people I might meet, the activities of the Yiddish anarchists, and other interesting matters. I was grateful to my host, much more for his friendly concern and *camaraderie* than for the tea and cake. I forgot the bitterness that had filled my soul over the cruel reception given me by my own kin. New York no longer seemed the monster it had appeared in the endless hours of my painful walk on the Bowery.

Later Solotaroff took me to Sachs's café on Suffolk Street, which, as he informed me, was the headquarters of the East Side radicals, socialists, and anarchists, as well as of the young Yiddish writers and poets. "Everybody forgathers there," he remarked; "the Minkin sisters will no doubt also be there."

For one who had just come away from the monotony of a provincial town like Rochester and whose nerves were on edge from a night's trip in a stuffy car, the noise and turmoil that greeted us at Sachs's were certainly not very soothing. The place consisted of two rooms and was packed. Everybody talked, gesticulated, and argued, in Yiddish and Russian, each competing with the other. I was almost overcome in this strange human medley. My escort discovered two girls at a table. He introduced them as Anna and Helen Minkin.

They were Russian Jewish working girls. Anna, the older, was about my own age; Helen perhaps eighteen. Soon we came to an understanding about my living with them, and my anxiety and uncertainty were over. I had a roof over my head; I had found friends. The bedlam at Sachs's no longer mattered. I began to breathe freer, to feel less of an alien.

While the four of us were having our dinner, and Solotaroff was pointing out to me the different people in the café, I suddenly heard a powerful voice call: "Extra-large steak! Extra cup of coffee!" My own capital was so small and the need for economy so great that I was startled by such apparent extravagance. Besides, Solotaroff had told me that only poor students, writers, and workers were the clients of Sachs. I wondered who that reckless person could be and how he could afford such food. "Who is that glutton?" I asked. Solotaroff laughed aloud. "That is Alexander Berkman. He can eat for three. But he rarely has enough money for much food. When he has, he eats Sachs out of his supplies. I'll introduce him to you."

We had finished our meal, and several people came to our table to talk to Solotaroff. The man of the extra-large steak was still packing it away as if he had gone hungry for weeks. Just as we were about to depart, he approached us, and Solotaroff introduced him. He was no more than a boy, hardly eighteen, but with the neck and chest of a giant. His jaw was strong, made more pronounced by his thick lips. His face was almost severe, but for his high, studious forehead and intelligent eyes. A determined youngster, I thought. Presently Berkman remarked to me: "Johann Most is speaking tonight. Do you want to come to hear him?"

How extraordinary, I thought, that on my very first day in New York I should have the chance to behold with my own eyes and hear the fiery man whom the Rochester press used to portray as the personification of the devil, a criminal, a bloodthirsty demon! I had planned to visit Most in the office of his newspaper some time later, but that the opportunity should present itself in such an unexpected manner gave me the feeling that something wonderful was about to happen, something that would decide the whole course of my life.

W. D. HOWELLS
(1837–1920)

Often referred to as the 'Dean of American Letters', W. D. Howells left an expansive mark on American literature. In novels such as *The Rise of Silas Lapham* (1885) and *An Imperative Duty* (1891), he offered readers incisive and often humorous slices of late-nineteenth-century American life and its dilemmas. As editor of the *Atlantic Monthly* magazine, he championed a generation of realist writers, including Sarah Orne Jewett, Stephen Crane and Charles Chesnutt. By birth a 'Westerner' from Ohio, Howells lived for a number of years in Boston before moving to New York City in 1899. His affection for the everyday sights and sounds of the city, which he regularly took in from benches in Washington Square Park and the back corners of Italian restaurants, surfaced in both letters to writer friends such as Henry James and the sketches of modern urban life he integrated into his fiction. In this selection from his 1889 novel, *A Hazard of New Fortunes*, Howells offers a memorable (and still quite familiar) take on the experience of apartment hunting in New York through the eyes of a middle-aged Bostonian couple newly arrived in the metropolis.

from A Hazard of New Fortunes

Mrs. March took the vertebrate with her to the Vienna Coffee-house, where they went to breakfast next morning. She made March buy her the *Herald* and the *World*, and she added to its spiny convolutions from them. She read the new advertisements aloud with ardour and with faith to believe that the apartments described in them were every one truthfully represented, and that any one of them was richly responsive to their needs. "Elegant, light, large, single, and outside flats" were offered with "all improvements—bath, ice-box, etc."— for $25 and $30 a month. The cheapness was amazing. The Wagram, the Esmeralda, the Jacinth, advertised them for $40 and $60, "with steam-heat and elevator," rent free till November. Others, attractive from their air of conscientious scruple, announced "first-class flats; good order; reasonable rents." The Helena asked the reader if she had seen the "cabinet finish, hard-wood floors, and frescoed ceilings" of its $50 flats; the Asteroid affirmed that such apartments, with "six light rooms and bath, porcelain wash-tubs, electric bells, and hall-boy," as it offered for $75 were unapproached by competition. There was a sameness in the jargon which tended to confusion. Mrs. March got several flats on her list which promised neither steam-heat nor elevators; she forgot herself so far as to include two or three as remote from the down-town region of her choice as

Harlem. But after she had rejected these the nondescript vertebrate was still voluminous enough to sustain her buoyant hopes.

The waiter, who remembered them from year to year, had put them at a window giving a pretty good section of Broadway, and before they set out on their search they had a moment of reminiscence. They recalled the Broadway of five, of ten, of twenty years ago, swelling and roaring with a tide of gaily painted omnibuses and of picturesque traffic that the horse-cars have now banished from it. The grind of their wheels and the clash of their harsh bells imperfectly fill the silence that the omnibuses have left, and the eye misses the tumultuous perspective of former times.

They went out and stood for a moment before Grace Church, and looked down the stately thorough-fare, and found it no longer impressive, no longer characteristic. It is still Broadway in name, but now it is like any other street. You do not now take your life in your hand when you attempt to cross it; the Broadway policeman who supported the elbow of timorous beauty in the hollow of his cotton-gloved palm and guided its little fearful boots over the crossing, while he arrested the billowy omnibuses on either side with an imperious glance, is gone, and all that certain processional, barbaric gaiety of the place is gone.

"Palmyra, Baalbec, Timour of the Desert," said March, voicing their common feeling of the change.

They turned and went into the beautiful church, and found themselves in time for the matin service. Rapt far from New York, if not from earth, in the dim richness of the painted light, the hallowed music took them with solemn ecstasy; the aërial, aspiring Gothic forms seemed to lift them heavenward. They came out, reluctant, into the dazzle and bustle of the street, with a feeling that they were too good for it, which they confessed to each other with whimsical consciousness.

"But no matter how consecrated we feel now," he said, "we mustn't forget that we went into the church for precisely the same reason that we went to the Vienna Café for breakfast—to gratify an æsthetic sense, to renew the faded pleasure of travel for a moment, to get back into the Europe of our youth. It was a purely Pagan impulse, Isabel, and we'd better own it."

"I don't know," she returned. "I think we reduce ourselves to the bare bones too much. I wish we didn't always recognise the facts as we do. Sometimes I should like to blink them. I should like to think I was devouter than I am, and younger and prettier."

'Better not; you couldn't keep it up. Honesty is the best policy even in such things."

"No; I don't like it, Basil. I should rather wait till the last day for some of my motives to come to the top. I know they're always mixed, but do let me give them the benefit of a doubt sometimes."

"Well, well, have it your own way, my dear. But I prefer not to lay up so many disagreeable surprises for myself at that time."

She would not consent. "I know I am a good deal younger than I was. I feel quite in the mood of that morning when we walked down Broadway on our wedding journey. Don't you?"

"Oh yes. But I know I'm not younger; I'm only prettier."

She laughed for pleasure in his joke, and also for unconscious joy in the gay New York weather, in which there was no *arrière pensée* of the east wind. They had crossed Broadway, and were walking over to Washington Square, in the region of which they now hoped to place themselves. The *primo tenore* statue of Garibaldi had already taken possession of the place in the name of Latin progress, and they met Italian faces, French faces, Spanish faces, as they strolled over the asphalte walks, under the thinning shadows of the autumn-stricken sycamores. They met the familiar picturesque raggedness of southern Europe with the old kindly illusion that somehow it existed for their appreciation, and that it found adequate compensation for poverty in this. March thought he sufficiently expressed his tacit sympathy in sitting down on one of the iron benches with his wife, and letting a little Neapolitan put a superfluous shine on his boots, while their desultory comment wandered with equal esteem to the old-fashioned American respectability which keeps the north side of the square in vast mansions of red brick, and the international shabbiness which has invaded the southern border, and broken it up into lodging-houses, shops, beer gardens, and studios.

They noticed the sign of an apartment to let on the north side, and as soon as the little boot-black could be bought off they went over to look at it. The janitor met them at the door and examined them. Then he said, as if still in doubt, "It has ten rooms, and the rent is twenty-eight hundred dollars."

"It wouldn't do, then," March replied, and left him to divide the responsibility between the paucity of the rooms and the enormity of the rent as he best might. But their self-love had received a wound, and they questioned each other what it was in their appearance made him doubt their ability to pay so much.

"Of course we don't look like New-Yorkers," sighed Mrs. March, "and we've walked through the Square. That might be as if we had walked along the Park Street mall in the Common before we came out on Beacon. Do you suppose he could have seen you getting your boots blacked in that way?"

"It's useless to ask," said March. "But I never can recover from this blow."

"Oh pshaw! You know you hate such things as badly as I do. It was very impertinent of him."

"Let us go back, and *écraser l'infâme* by paying him a year's rent in advance and taking immediate possession. Nothing else can soothe my wounded feelings. *You* were not having your boots blacked: why shouldn't he have supposed you were a New-Yorker, and I a country cousin?"

"They always know. Don't you remember Mrs. Williams's going to a Fifth Avenue milliner in a Worth dress, and the woman's asking her instantly what hotel she should send her hat to?"

"Yes; these things drive one to despair. I don't wonder the bodies of so many genteel strangers are found in the waters around New York. Shall we try the south side, my dear? or had we better go back to our rooms and rest a while?"

Mrs. March had out the vertebrate, and was consulting one of its glittering ribs, and glancing up from it at a house before which they stood. "Yes, it's the number; but do they call *this* being ready October 1st?" The little area in front of the basement was heaped with a mixture of mortar, bricks, laths, and shavings from the interior; the brown-stone steps to the front door were similarly bestrewn; the doorway showed the half-open rough pine carpenter's hatch of an unfinished house; the sashless windows of every story showed the activity of workmen within; the clatter of hammers and the hiss of saws came out to them from every opening.

"They may call it October 1st," said March, "because it's too late to contradict them. But they'd better not call it December 1st in *my* presence; I'll let them say January 1st, at a pinch."

"We will go in and look at it anyway," said his wife; and he admired how, when she was once within, she began provisionally to settle the family in each of the several floors with the female instinct for domiciliation which never failed her. She had the help of the landlord, who was present to urge forward the workmen apparently; he lent a hopeful fancy to the solution of all her questions. To get her from under his influence March had to represent that the place was damp from undried plastering, and that if she stayed she would probably be down with that New York pneumonia which visiting Bostonians are always dying of. Once safely on the pavement outside, she realised that the apartment was not only unfinished, but unfurnished, and had neither steam-heat nor elevator. "But I thought we had better look at everything," she explained.

"Yes, but not take everything. If I hadn't pulled you away from there by main force you'd have not only died of New York pneumonia on the spot, but you'd have had us all settled there before we knew what we were about."

"Well, that's what I can't help, Basil. It's the only way I can realise whether it will do for us. I have to dramatise the whole thing."

She got a deal of pleasure as well as excitement out of this, and he had to own that the process of setting up house-keeping in so many different places was not only entertaining, but tended, through association with their first beginnings in house-keeping, to restore the image of their early married days, and to make them young again.

It went on all day, and continued far into the night, until it was too late to go to the theatre, too late to do anything but tumble into bed and simultaneously fall on sleep. They groaned over their reiterated disappointments, but they could not deny that the interest was unfailing, and that they got a great deal of fun out of it all. Nothing could abate Mrs. March's faith in her advertisements. One of them sent her to a flat of ten rooms which promised to be the solution of all their difficulties; it proved to be over a livery-stable, a liquor store, and a milliner's shop, none of the first fashion. Another led them far into old Greenwich Village to an apartment-house, which she refused to enter behind a small girl with a loaf of bread under one arm and a quart can of milk under the other.

In their search they were obliged, as March complained, to the acquisition of useless information in a degree unequalled in their experience. They came to excel in the sad knowledge of the line at which respectability distinguishes itself from shabbiness. Flattering advertisements took them to numbers of huge apartment-houses chiefly distinguishable from tenement-houses by the absence of fire-escapes on their façades, till Mrs. March refused to stop at any door where there were more than six bell-ratchets and speaking-tubes on either hand. Before the middle of the afternoon she decided against ratchets altogether, and confined herself to knobs, neatly set in the door-trim. Her husband was still sunk in the superstition that you can live anywhere you like in New York, and he would have paused at some places where her quicker eye caught the fatal sign of "Modes" in the ground-floor windows. She found that there was an east and west line beyond which they could not go if they wished to keep their self-respect, and that within the region to which they had restricted themselves there was a choice of streets. At first all the New York streets looked to them ill-paved, dirty, and repulsive; the general infamy imparted itself in their casual impression to streets in no wise guilty. But they began to notice that some streets were quiet and clean, and, though never so quiet and clean as Boston streets, that they wore an air of encouraging reform, and suggested a future of greater and greater domesticity. Whole blocks of these down-town cross streets seemed to have been redeemed from decay, and even in the midst of squalor a dwelling here and there had been seized, painted a dull-red as to its brickwork, and a glossy black as to its wood-work, and with a bright brass bell-pull and door knob and a large brass plate for its key-hole escutcheon, had been endowed with an effect of purity and pride which removed its shabby neighbourhood far from it.

Some of these houses were quite small, and imaginably within their means; but, as March said, somebody seemed always to be living there himself, and the fact that none of them were to rent kept Mrs. March true to her ideal of a flat. Nothing prevented its realisation so much as its difference from the New York ideal of a flat, which was inflexibly seven rooms and a bath. One or two rooms might be at the front, the rest crooked and cornered backward through increasing and then decreasing darkness till they reached a light bedroom or kitchen at the rear. It might be the one or the other, but it was always the seventh room with the bath; or if, as sometimes happened, it was the eighth, it was so after having counted the bath as one. In this case the janitor said you always counted the bath as one. If the flats were advertised as having "all light rooms," he explained that any room with a window giving into the open air of a court or shaft was counted a light room.

The Marches tried to make out why it was that these flats were so much more repulsive than the apartments which every one lived in abroad; but they could only do so upon the supposition that in their European days they were too young, too happy, too full of the future, to notice whether rooms were inside or outside, light or dark, big or little, high or low. "Now we're imprisoned in the present," he said, "and we have to make the worst of it."

He could see that she had got to the end of her nervous strength for the present, and he proposed that they should take the Elevated road as far as it would carry them into the country, and shake off their nightmare of flat-hunting for an hour or two; but her conscience would not let her. She convicted him of levity equal to that of the New-Yorkers in proposing such a thing; and they dragged through the day. She was too tired to care for dinner, and in the night she had a dream from which she woke herself with a cry that roused him too. It was something about the children at first, whom they had talked of wistfully before falling asleep, and then it was of a hideous thing with two square eyes and a series of sections growing darker and then lighter, till the tail of the monstrous articulate was quite luminous again. She shuddered at the vague description she was able to give; but he asked, "Did it offer to bite you?"

"No. That was the most frightful thing about it; it had no mouth."

March laughed. "Why, my dear, it was nothing but a harmless New York flat—seven rooms and a bath."

"I really believe it was," she consented, recognising an architectural resemblance, and she fell asleep again, and woke renewed for the work before them.

Theodore Dreiser
(1871–1945)

Born in Terre Haute, Indiana, to an impoverished German American family, Theodore Dreiser was a gifted and largely self-taught writer who authored some of America's most influential works of naturalist fiction, including *Sister Carrie* (1900) and *An American Tragedy* (1925). His unflinching eye on the social and economic turmoil of his time and frank depictions of then-taboo topics such as sex won him an Award of Merit from the American Academy of Letters and a posthumous induction into the Chicago Literary Hall of Fame, as well as the ire of would-be censors in the US at the turn of the century and in Germany under the Nazi regime. But, while he got his start at writing at the *Chicago Globe*, he launched his career as a novelist after he moved to New York in 1894 to work as editor of *Ev'ry Month* magazine. This selection from his debut novel, *Sister Carrie*, follows a middle-aged Midwestern businessman and his young mistress on their scandalous arrival to New York, reflecting on the dreams they bring with them, the city already saturated with other such schemers and dreamers and the dazzling standard-issue modern conveniences awaiting them in their new Upper West Side apartment.

from Sister Carrie

Whatever a man like Hurstwood could be in Chicago, it is very evident that he would be but an inconspicuous drop in an ocean like New York. In Chicago, whose population still ranged about 500,000, millionaires were not numerous. The rich had not become so conspicuously rich as to drown all moderate incomes in obscurity. The attention of the inhabitants was not so distracted by local celebrities in the dramatic, artistic, social, and religious fields as to shut the well-positioned man from view. In Chicago the two roads to distinction were politics and trade. In New York the roads were any one of a half-hundred, and each had been diligently pursued by hundreds, so that celebrities were numerous. The sea was already full of whales. A common fish must needs disappear wholly from view—remain unseen. In other words, Hurstwood was nothing.

There is a more subtle result of such a situation as this, which, though not always taken into account, produces the tragedies of the world. The great create an atmosphere which reacts badly upon the small. This atmosphere is easily and quickly felt. Walk among the magnificent residences, the splendid equipages, the gilded shops, restaurants, resorts of all kinds; scent the flowers, the silks, the wines; drink of the laughter springing from the soul of luxurious content, of the glances which gleam like light from defiant spears; feel the quality of the smiles which cut like glistening swords and of strides born of place, and you shall know of what is the atmosphere of the high and mighty. Little use to argue that of such is not the kingdom of greatness, but so long as the world is attracted by this and the human heart views this as the one desirable realm which it must attain, so long, to that heart, will this remain the realm of greatness. So long, also, will the atmosphere of this realm work its desperate results in the soul of man. It is like a chemical reagent. One day of it, like one drop of the other, will so affect and discolour the views, the aims, the desire of the mind, that it will thereafter remain forever dyed. A day of it to the untried mind is like opium to the untried body. A craving is set up which, if gratified, shall eternally result in dreams and death. Aye! dreams unfulfilled—gnawing, luring, idle phantoms which beckon and lead, beckon and lead, until death and dissolution dissolve their power and restore us blind to nature's heart.

A man of Hurstwood's age and temperament is not subject to the illusions and burning desires of youth, but neither has he the strength of hope which gushes as a fountain in the heart of youth. Such an atmosphere could not incite in him the cravings of a boy of eighteen, but in so far as they were excited, the lack of hope made them proportionately bitter. He could not fail to notice the signs of affluence and luxury on every hand. He had been to New York before and knew the resources of its folly. In part it was an awesome place to him, for here gathered all that he most respected on this earth—wealth, place, and fame. The majority of the celebrities with whom he had tipped glasses in his day as manager hailed from this self-centred and populous spot. The most inviting stories of pleasure and luxury had been told of places and individuals here. He knew it to be true that unconsciously he was brushing elbows with fortune the livelong day; that a hundred or five hundred thousand gave no one the privilege of living more than comfortably in so wealthy a place. Fashion and pomp required more ample sums, so that the poor man was nowhere. All this he realised, now quite sharply, as he faced the city, cut off from his friends, despoiled of his modest fortune, and even his name, and forced to begin the battle for place and comfort all over again. He was not old, but he was not so dull but that he could feel he soon would be. Of a sudden, then, this show of fine clothes, place, and power took on peculiar significance. It was emphasised by contrast with his own distressing state.

And it was distressing. He soon found that freedom from fear of arrest was not the *sine qua non* of his existence. That danger dissolved, the next necessity became the grievous thing. The paltry sum of thirteen hundred and some odd dollars set against the need of rent, clothing, food, and pleasure for years to come was a spectacle little calculated to induce peace of mind in one who had been accustomed to spend five times that sum in the course of a year. He thought upon the subject rather actively the first few days he was in New York, and decided that he must act quickly. As a consequence, he consulted the business opportunities advertised in the morning papers and began investigations on his own account.

That was not before he had become settled, however. Carrie and he went looking for a flat, as arranged, and found one in Seventy-eighth Street near Amsterdam Avenue. It was a five-story building, and their flat was on the third floor. Owing to the fact that the street was not yet built up solidly, it was possible to see east to the green tops of the trees in Central Park and west to the broad waters of the Hudson, a glimpse of which was to be had out of the west windows. For the privilege of six rooms and a bath, running in a straight line, they were compelled to pay thirty-five dollars a month—an average, and yet exorbitant, rent for a home at the time. Carrie noticed the difference between the size of the rooms here and in Chicago and mentioned it.

"You'll not find anything better, dear," said Hurstwood, "unless you go into one of the old-fashioned houses, and then you won't have any of these conveniences."

Carrie picked out the new abode because of its newness and bright wood-work. It was one of the very new ones supplied with steam heat, which was a great advantage. The stationary range, hot and cold water, dumb-waiter, speaking tubes, and call-bell for the janitor pleased her very much. She had enough of the instincts of a housewife to take great satisfaction in these things.

Hurstwood made arrangement with one of the

instalment houses whereby they furnished the flat complete and accepted fifty dollars down and ten dollars a month. He then had a little plate, bearing the name G. W. Wheeler, made, which he placed on his letter-box in the hall. It sounded exceedingly odd to Carrie to be called Mrs. Wheeler by the janitor, but in time she became used to it and looked upon the name as her own.

JAMES WELDON JOHNSON
(1871–1938)

Pioneering educator, lawyer, diplomat, activist and writer James Weldon Johnson was the first African American professor to be appointed at New York University. He was also a leading figure in the NAACP, in which capacity he fought voter suppression in the South and was instrumental in both its legal casework and growth as a leading civil rights advocacy organization. But Johnson began his professional life in musical theatre, moving to New York in 1901 to embark on a career as a songwriter. He authored more than two hundred Broadway songs with his brother, J. Rosamund Johnson, as well as the hymn 'Lift Every Voice and Sing' (1900), which became known as the Black national anthem, and several landmark works of African American poetry, fiction and sociology, including *God's Trombones: Seven Negro Sermons in Verse* (1927), *Black Manhattan* (1930) and his groundbreaking 1922 anthology, *The Book of American Negro Poetry*. In this selection from his debut novel, *The Autobiography of an Ex-Colored Man* (1912), Johnson offers readers the sights and ragtime sounds of New York as glimpsed through the eyes of a young African American man who has just arrived from the South.

from The Autobiography of an Ex-Colored Man

We steamed up into New York harbor late one afternoon in spring. The last efforts of the sun were being put forth in turning the waters of the bay to glistening gold; the green islands on either side, in spite of their warlike mountings, looked calm and peaceful; the buildings of the town shone out in a reflected light which gave the city an air of enchantment; and, truly, it is an enchanted spot. New York City is the most fatally fascinating thing in America. She sits like a great witch at the gate of the country, showing her alluring white face, and hiding her crooked hands and feet under the folds of her wide garments,—constantly enticing thousands from far within, and tempting those who come from across the seas to go no farther. And all these become the victims of her caprice. Some she at once crushes beneath her cruel feet; others she condemns to a fate like that of galley slaves; a few she favors and fondles, riding them high on the bubbles of fortune; then with a sudden breath she blows the bubbles out and laughs mockingly as she watches them fall.

Twice I had passed through it; but this was really my first visit to New York; and as I walked about that evening I began to feel the dread power of the city; the crowds, the lights, the excitement, the gayety and all its subtler stimulating influences began to take effect upon me. My blood ran quicker, and I felt that I was just beginning to live. To some natures this stimulant of life in a great city becomes a thing as binding and necessary as opium is to one addicted to the habit. It becomes their breath of life; they cannot exist outside of it; rather than be deprived of it they are content to suffer hunger, want, pain and misery; they would not exchange even a ragged and wretched condition among the great crowd for any degree of comfort away from it.

As soon as we landed, four of us went directly to a lodging-house in 27th Street, just west of Sixth Avenue. When we had become located we went out and got supper; then walked around until about ten o'clock. At that hour we met a couple of young fellows who lived in New York and were known to one of the members of our party. It was suggested we go to a certain place which was known by the proprietor's name. We turned into one of the cross streets and mounted the stoop of a house in about the middle of a block between Sixth and Seventh Avenues. One of the young men whom we had met rang a bell, and a man on the inside cracked the door a couple of inches; then opened it and let us in. We found ourselves in the hallway of what had once been a residence. The front parlor had been converted into a bar, and a half dozen or so of well dressed men were in the room. We went in, and after a general introduction had several rounds of beer. In the back parlor a crowd was sitting and standing around the walls of the room watching an exciting and noisy game of pool. I walked back and joined this crowd to watch the game, and principally to get away from the drinking party. The game was really interesting, the players being quite expert, and the excitement was heightened by the bets which were being made on the result. At times the antics and remarks of both players and spectators were amusing. When, at a critical point, a player missed a shot he was deluged by those financially interested in his making it with a flood of epithets synonymous to "chump"; while from the others he would be jeered by such remarks as "N, dat cue ain't no hoe-handle." I noticed that among this class of colored men the word "n" was freely used in about the same sense as the word "fellow," and sometimes as a term of almost endearment; but I soon learned that its use was positively and absolutely prohibited to white men.

I stood watching this pool game until I was called by my friends, who were still in the bar-room, to go upstairs. On the second floor there were two large rooms. From the hall I looked into the one on the front. There was a large, round table in the center, at which five or six men were seated playing poker. The air and conduct here were greatly in contrast to what I had just seen in the pool-room; these men were evidently the aristocrats of the place; they were well, perhaps a bit flashily, dressed and spoke in low modulated voices, frequently using the word "gentlemen"; in fact, they seemed to be practicing a sort of Chesterfieldian politeness towards each other. I was watching these men with a great deal of interest and some degree of admiration, when I was again called by the members of our party, and I followed them on to the back room. There was a door-keeper at this room, and we were admitted only after inspection. When we got inside I saw a crowd of men of all ages and kinds grouped about an old billiard table, regarding some of whom, in supposing them to be white, I made no mistake. At first I did not know what these men were doing; they were using terms that were strange to me. I could hear only a confusion of voices exclaiming, "Shoot the two!" "Shoot the four!" "Fate me!" "Fate me!" "I've got you fated!" "Twenty-five cents he don't turn!" This was the ancient and terribly fascinating game of dice, popularly known as "craps." I, myself, had played pool in Jacksonville; it is a favorite game among cigar-makers, and I had seen others play cards; but here was something new. I edged my way in to the table and stood between one of my new-found New York friends and a tall, slender, black fellow, who was making side bets while the dice were at the other end of the table. My companion explained to me the principles of the game; and they are so simple that they hardly need to be explained twice. The dice came around the table until they reached the man on the other side of the tall, black fellow. He lost, and the latter said, "Gimme the bones." He threw a dollar on the table and said, "Shoot the dollar." His style of play was so strenuous that he had to be allowed plenty of room. He shook the dice high above his head, and each time he threw them on the table he emitted a grunt such as men give when they are putting forth physical exertion with a rhythmic regularity. He frequently whirled completely around on his heels, throwing the dice the entire length of the table, and talking to them as though they were trained animals. He appealed to them in short singsong phrases. "Come dice," he would say. "Little Phoebe," "Little Joe," "Way down yonder in the cornfield." Whether these mystic incantations were efficacious or not I could not say, but, at any rate, his luck was great, and he had what gamblers term "nerve." "Shoot the dollar!" "Shoot the two!" "Shoot the four!" "Shoot the eight!" came from his lips as quickly as the dice turned to his advantage. My companion asked me if I had ever played. I told him no. He said that I ought to try my luck; that everybody won at first. The tall man at my side was waving his arms in the air exclaiming "Shoot the sixteen!" "Shoot the sixteen!" "Fate me!" Whether it was my companion's suggestion or some latent dare-devil strain in my blood which suddenly sprang into activity I do not know; but with a thrill of excitement which went through my whole body I threw a twenty dollar bill on the table and said in a trembling voice, "I fate you."

I could feel that I had gained the attention and respect of everybody in the room, every eye was fixed on me, and the widespread question, "Who is he?" went around. This was gratifying to a certain sense of vanity of which I have never been able to rid myself, and I felt that it was worth the money even if I lost. The tall man with a whirl on his heels and a double grunt threw the dice; four was the number which turned up. This is considered as a hard "point" to make. He redoubled his contortions and his grunts and his pleadings to the dice; but on his third or fourth throw the fateful seven turned up, and I had won. My companion and all my friends shouted to me to follow up my luck. The fever was on me. I seized the dice. My hands were so hot that the bits of bone felt like pieces of ice. I shouted as loudly as I could, "Shoot it all!" but the blood was tingling so about my ears that I could not hear my own voice. I was soon "fated." I threw the dice—seven—I had won. "Shoot it all!" I cried again. There was a pause; the stake was more than one man cared to or could cover. I was finally "fated" by several men taking "a part" of it. I then threw the dice again. Seven. I had won. "Shoot it all!" I shouted excitedly. After a short delay I was "fated." Again I rolled the dice. Eleven. Again I had won. My friends now surrounded me and, much against my inclination, forced me to take down all of the money except five dollars. I tried my luck once more, and threw some small "Point" which I failed to make, and the dice passed on to the next man.

In less than three minutes I had won more than two hundred dollars, a sum which afterwards cost me dearly. I was the hero of the moment, and was soon surrounded by a group of men who expressed admiration for my "nerve" and predicted for me a brilliant future as a gambler. Although at the time I had no thought of becoming a gambler I felt proud of my success.

On passing downstairs I was told that the third and top floor of the house was occupied by the proprietor. When we passed through the bar I treated everybody in the room,—and that was no small number, for eight or ten had followed us down. Then our party went out. It was now about half-past twelve, but my nerves were at such a tension that I could not endure the mere thought of going to bed. I asked if there was no other place to which we could go; our guides said yes, and suggested that we go to the "Club." We went to Sixth Avenue, walked two blocks, and turned to the west into another street. We stopped in front of a house with three stories and a basement. In the basement was a Chinese Chopsuey restaurant. There was a red lantern at the iron gate to the areaway, inside of which the Chinaman's name was printed. We went up the steps of the stoop, rang the bell, and were admitted without any delay. From the outside the house bore a rather gloomy aspect, the windows being absolutely dark, but within it was a veritable house of mirth. When we had passed through a small vestibule and reached the hallway we heard mingled sounds of music and laughter, the clink of glasses and the pop of bottles. We went into the main room, and I was little prepared for what I saw. The brilliancy of the place, the display of diamond rings, scarf-pins, ear-rings and breast-pins, the big rolls of money that were brought into evidence when drinks were paid for, and the air of gayety that pervaded, all completely dazzled and dazed me. I felt positively giddy, and it was several minutes before I was able to make any clear and definite observations.

We at length secured places at a table in a corner of the room, and as soon as we could attract the attention of one of the busy waiters ordered a round of drinks. When I had somewhat collected my senses I realized that in a large back room into which the main room opened, there was a young fellow singing a song, accompanied on the piano by a short, thick-set, dark man. Between each verse he did some dance steps, which brought forth great applause and a shower of small coins at his feet. After the singer had responded to a rousing encore, the stout man at the piano began to run his fingers up and down the keyboard. This he did in a manner which indicated that he was master of a good deal of technic. Then he began to play; and such playing! I stopped talking to listen. It was music of a kind I had never heard before. It was music that demanded physical response, patting of the feet, drumming of the fingers, or nodding of the head in time with the beat. The barbaric harmonies, the audacious resolutions often consisting of an abrupt jump from one key to another, the intricate rhythms in which the accents fell in the most unexpected places, but in which the beat was never lost, produced a most curious effect. And, too, the player,—the dexterity of his left hand in making rapid octave runs and jumps was little short of marvelous; and, with his right hand, he frequently swept half the keyboard with clean cut chromatics which he fitted in so nicely as never to fail to arouse in his listeners a sort of pleasant surprise at the accomplishment of the feat.

This was ragtime music, then a novelty in New York, and just growing to be a rage which has not yet subsided.

I became so interested in both the music and the player that I left the table where I was sitting, and made my way through the hall into the back room, where I could see as well as hear. I talked to the piano player between the musical numbers, and found out that he was just a natural musician, never having taken a lesson in his life. Not only could he play almost anything he heard, but could accompany singers in songs he had never heard. He had by ear alone, composed some pieces, several of which he played over for me; each of them was properly proportioned and balanced. I began to wonder what this man with such a lavish natural endowment would have done had he been trained. Perhaps he wouldn't have done anything at all; he might have become, at best, a mediocre imitator of the great masters in what they have already done to a finish, or one of the modern innovators who strive after originality by seeing how cleverly they can dodge about through the rules of harmony, and at the same time avoid melody. It is certain that he would not have been so delightful as he was in ragtime.

I sat by watching and listening to this man until I was dragged away by my friends. The place was now almost deserted; only a few stragglers hung on, and they were all the worse for drink. My friends were well up in this class. We passed into the street; the lamps were pale against the sky; day was just breaking. We went home and got into bed. I fell into a fitful sort of sleep with ragtime music ringing continually in my ears.

ANAÏS NIN
(1903–1977)

Franco-American writer Anaïs Nin was many things during her lifetime: a path-breaking experimental novelist and writer of short stories and erotica; a daring diarist; a muse, benefactor and confidante to a number of leading twentieth-century writers, including Henry Miller and Gore Vidal; a psychoanalyst in training; a gifted letterpress printer; and, in the final years of her life, a feminist icon for her bold, unapologetic depictions of female desire. Born in a suburb of Paris to Catalan-Cuban parents, Nin spent her childhood moving between Barcelona, Paris, Havana and New York. She launched her literary career from Paris with the publication of *D. H. Lawrence: An Unprofessional Study* (1932), but she settled in New York City in 1940, on the eve of the German invasion of Paris, to pursue her psychoanalytic training, and lived in the US for the rest of her life. In this letter, written during a brief stint in New York in the early 1930s, Nin revels in the tempo and vitality of this city that she drinks up with such gusto.

Letter to Henry Miller

> Barbizon Plaza Hotel
> 6th Ave & 58th St
> Dec 3, 1934

[Henry:]

I rushed you a note the other day and have not been able to write a line for myself since. Have let things take their course and since making money for the rent was the first item on the list I accepted the enormous amount of work required by the [Psychological] Center. Next weekend I see about the dancing. Meanwhile, I'm busy all day, like a big business woman, and then every night somebody says: "Let us show you New York." Americans are like Spaniards. So I have seen shows, Broadway, lunch on top of the Empire State, a dance hall in Harlem, movies at Radio City. I'm in love with N.Y. It matches my mood. I'm not overwhelmed. It is the suitable scene for my ever ever heightened life. I love the proportions, the amplitude, the brilliance, the polish, the solidity. I look up at Radio City insolently and love it. It is all great, and Babylonian, Broadway at night, Cellophane. The newness. The vitality. True, it is only physical. But it's inspiring. Just bring your own contents, and you create a sparkle of the highest power I'm not moved, not speechless. I stand straight, tough, and I meet the impact. I feel the glow and the dancing in everything. The radio music in the taxis, scientific magic, which can all be used lyrically. That's my last word. Give New York to a poet. He can use it. It can be poetized. Or maybe that's a mania of mine, to poetize. I live lightly, smoothly, actively, ears and eyes wide open, alert, oiled! I feel a kind of exhilaration and the tempo is like that of my blood. I'm at once beyond, over and in New York, tasting it fully.

I don't know if I am telling you enough. I write you between telephone calls, visitors, letters etc. I don't hear myself writing. The only missing element is time. It is rare! We are flying. One goes for the weekend to Washington. One flies to Chicago in four hours. Rank has to go for lectures all over, and leaves me charge. A ship "scalp" gave me Frieda's book on Lawrence [*Not I, But the wind* . . .]. I can't read it. Saying it for you. But here is the rent check. Are you happy?

The telephone is at my elbow. Any day I may be idle, then I call up Emil [Schnellock] or I walk through Brooklyn.

Write me at the Barbizon. They never send up the mail. I call for it. It is quite safe.

A.

MISERY AND THE METROPOLIS

Charles Dickens
(1812–1870)

Charles Dickens authored some of the still most celebrated and widely read classics of nineteenth-century British literature, including *Oliver Twist* (1838), *A Christmas Carol* (1843) and *Great Expectations* (1861), works which continue to resonate with contemporary readers and garner additional audiences through ongoing adaptations for film and TV. Born in Portsmouth and raised in Kent and, later, London, Dickens's childhood was deeply marked by his father's time in a debtors' prison and his own experience, aged twelve, of unrelenting factory work to support his mother and siblings – and he continued to bring a sharp, often satirical eye to the grinding effects of poverty and child labour across his voluminous body of writings, despite the extraordinary literary celebrity he achieved during his lifetime. In this selection from an essay written during his first visit to New York and first trip to America in 1842, Dickens turns his readers' attention, and his inimitably acerbic wit, to the rapid fortunes made on the New York's stock exchange, and the inmates he encounters nearby in the city's then newly built municipal prison (commonly known as 'the Tombs').

from American Notes

This narrow thoroughfare, baking and blistering in the sun, is Wall Street: the Stock Exchange and Lombard Street of New York. Many a rapid fortune has been made in this street, and many a no less rapid ruin. Some of these very merchants whom you see hanging about here now, have locked up money in their strong-boxes, like the man in the Arabian nights, and opening them again, have found but withered leaves. Below, here by the water side, where the bowsprits of ships stretch across the footway, and almost thrust themselves into the windows, lie the noble American vessels which have made their Packet Service the finest in the world. They have brought hither the foreigners who abound in all the streets: not, perhaps, that there are more here, than in other commercial cities; but elsewhere, they have particular haunts, and you must find them out; here, they pervade the town.

We must cross Broadway again; gaining some refreshment from the heat, in the sight of the great blocks of clean ice which are being carried into shops and bar-rooms; and the pine-apples and water-melons profusely displayed for sale. Fine streets of spacious houses here, you see!—Wall Street has furnished and dismantled many of them very often—and here a deep green leafy square. Be sure that is a hospitable house with inmates to be affectionately remembered always, where they have the open door and pretty show of plants within, and where the child with laughing eyes is peeping out of the window at the little dog below. You wonder what may be the use of this tall flagstaff in the by-street, with something like Liberty's head-dress on its top: so do I. But there is a passion for tall flagstaffs hereabouts, and you may see its twin brother in five minutes, if you have a mind.

Again across Broadway, and so—passing from the many colored crowd and glittering shops—into another long main street, the Bowery. A railroad yonder, see, where two stout horses trot along, drawing a score or two of people and a great wooden ark, with ease. The stores are poorer here; the passengers less gay. Clothes ready-made, and meat ready-cooked, are to be bought in these parts; and the lively whirl of carriages is exchanged for the deep rumble of carts and wagons. These signs which are so plentiful, in shape like river buoys, or small balloons, hoisted by cords to poles, and dangling there, announce, as you may see by looking up, "OYSTERS IN EVERY STYLE." They tempt the hungry most at night, for then dull candles glimmering inside, illuminate these dainty words, and make the mouths of idlers water, as they read and linger.

What is this dismal-fronted pile of bastard Egyptian, like an enchanter's palace in a melodrama!—a famous prison, called The Tombs. Shall we go in?

So. A long narrow lofty building, stove-heated as usual, with four galleries, one above the other, going round it, and communicating by stairs. Between the two sides of each gallery, and in its centre, a bridge, for the greater convenience of crossing. On each of these bridges sits a man: dozing or reading, or talking to an idle companion. On each tier, are two opposite rows of small iron doors. They look like furnace-doors, but are cold and black, as though the fires within had all gone out. Some two or three are open, and women, with drooping heads bent down, are talking to the inmates. The whole is lighted by a skylight, but it is fast closed; and from the roof there dangle, limp and drooping, two useless windsails.

A man with keys appears, to show us round. A good-looking fellow, and, in his way, civil and obliging.

"Are those black doors the cells?"

"Yes."

"Are they all full?"

"Well, they're pretty nigh full, and that's a fact, and no two ways about it."

"Those at the bottom are unwholesome, surely?"

"Why, we *do* only put colored people in 'em. That's the truth."

"When do the prisoners take exercise?"

"Well, they do without it pretty much."

"Do they never walk in the yard?"

"Considerable seldom."

"Sometimes, I suppose?"

"Well, it's rare they do. They keep pretty bright without it."

"But suppose a man were here for a twelvemonth. I know this is only a prison for criminals who are charged with grave offences, while they are awaiting their trial, or under remand, but the law here affords criminals many means of delay. What with motions for new trials, and in arrest of judgment, and what not, a prisoner might be here for twelve months, I take it, might he not?"

"Well, I guess he might."

"Do you mean to say that in all that time he would never come out at that little iron door, for exercise?"

"He might walk some, perhaps—not much."

"Will you open one of the doors?"

"All, if you like."

The fastenings jar and rattle, and one of the doors turns slowly on its hinges. Let us look in. A small bare cell, into which the light enters through a high chink in the wall. There is a rude means of washing, a table, and a bedstead. Upon the latter, sits a man of sixty; reading. He looks up for a moment; gives an impatient dogged shake; and fixes his eyes upon his book again. As we withdrew our heads, the door closes on him, and is fastened as before. This man has murdered his wife, and will probably be hanged.

"How long has he been here?"

"A month."

"When will he be tried?"

"Next term."

"When is that?"

"Next month."

"In England, if a man be under sentence of death,

even he has air and exercise at certain periods of the day."

"Possible?"

With what stupendous and untranslatable coolness he says this, and how loungingly he leads on to the women's side: making, as he goes, a kind of iron castanet of the key and the stair-rail!

Each cell door on this side has a square aperture in it. Some of the women peep anxiously through it at the sound of footsteps; others shrink away in shame.—For what offence can that lonely child, of ten or twelve years old, be shut up here? Oh! that boy? He is the son of the prisoner we saw just now; is a witness against his father; and is detained here for safe keeping, until the trial; that's all.

But it is a dreadful place for the child to pass the long days and nights in. This is rather hard treatment for a young witness, is it not?—What says our conductor?

"Well, it an't a very rowdy life, and *that's* a fact!"

Again he clinks his metal castanet, and leads us leisurely away. I have a question to ask him as we go.

"Pray, why do they call this place The Tombs?"

"Well, it's the cant name."

"I know it is. Why?"

"Some suicides happened here, when it was first built. I expect it come about from that."

"I saw just now, that that man's clothes were scattered about the floor of his cell. Don't you oblige the prisoners to be orderly, and put such things away?"

"Where should they put 'em?"

"Not on the ground surely. What do you say to hanging them up?"

He stops and looks round to emphasize his answer:

"Why, I say that's just it. When they had hooks they *would* hang themselves, so they're taken out of every cell, and there's only the marks left where they used to be!"

The prison-yard in which he pauses now, has been the scene of terrible performances. Into this narrow, grave-like place, men are brought out to die. The wretched creature stands beneath the gibbet on the ground; the rope about his neck; and when the sign is given, a weight at its other end comes running down, and swings him up into the air—a corpse.

The law requires that there be present at this dismal spectacle, the judge, the jury, and citizens to the amount of twenty-five. From the community it is hidden. To the dissolute and bad, the thing remains a frightful mystery. Between the criminal and them, the prison-wall is interposed as a thick gloomy veil. It is the curtain to his bed of death, his winding-sheet, and grave. From him it shuts out life, and all the motives to unrepenting hardihood in that last hour, which its mere sight and presence is often all sufficient to sustain. There are no bold eyes to make him bold; no ruffians to uphold a ruffian's name before. All beyond the pitiless stone wall, is unknown space.

Let us go forth again into the cheerful streets.

Once more in Broadway! Here are the same ladies in bright colors, walking to and fro, in pairs and singly;

yonder the very same light blue parasol which passed and repassed the hotel-window twenty times while we were sitting there. We are going to cross here. Take care of the Pigs. Two portly sows are trotting up behind this carriage, and a select party of half-a-dozen gentlemen hogs have just now turned the corner.

Louisa May Alcott
(1832–1888)

Raised in Concord and Boston in a household of staunch abolitionists and leading educational reformers, Louisa May Alcott is now best remembered for her classic American novel *Little Women*, the story of the four March girls that continues to captivate the imaginations of contemporary readers and filmmakers. But in her own day she was equally known for her unwavering support for women's rights, prison reform and temperance, as well as a remarkably wide body of literary works that spanned gothic tales, sketches of her time as a Civil War nurse, a biting satire of the Transcendental commune that her father helped to found, short stories for children and adults, fairy tales and novels. Alcott made a number of visits to New York to gather ideas for her stories and sketches, and drafted parts of *Little Women* while staying at her uncle's red-brick townhouse on MacDougal Street in the West Village. In this letter from the 1870s, she offers glimpses of the young paper boys navigating life on their own in the city and a hopeful account of the lodging house that New York reformers had built to give them a home.

Letter to Her Nephews

NEW YORK, Dec. 4, 1875.

Dear Fred and Donny,—We went to see the newsboys, and I wish you'd been with us, it was so interesting. A nice big house has been built for them, with dining-room and kitchen on the first floor, bath-rooms and school-room next, two big sleeping-places,—third and fourth stories,—and at the top a laundry and gymnasium. We saw all the tables set for breakfast,—a plate and bowl for each,—and in the kitchen great kettles, four times as big as our copper boiler, for tea and coffee, soup, and meat. They have bread and meat and coffee for breakfast, and bread and cheese and tea for supper, and get their own dinners out. School was just over when we got there, and one hundred and eighty boys were in the immense room with desks down the middle, and all around the walls were little cupboards numbered. Each boy on coming in gives his name, pays six cents, gets a key, and puts away his hat, books, and jacket (if he has 'em) in his own cubby for the night. They pay five cents for supper, and schooling, baths, etc., are free. They were a smart-looking set, larking round in shirts and trousers, barefooted, but the faces were clean, and the heads smooth, and clothes pretty decent; yet they support themselves, for not one of them has any parents or home but this. One little chap, only six, was trotting round as busy as a bee, locking up his small shoes and ragged jacket as if they were great treasures. I asked about little Pete, and the man told us his brother, only nine, supported him and took care of him entirely; and would n't let Pete be sent away to any home, because *he* wished to have "his family" with him.

Think of that, Fred! How would it seem to be all alone in a big city, with no mamma to cuddle you; no two grandpa's houses to take you in; not a penny but what you earned, and Donny to take care of? Could you do it? Nine-year-old Patsey does it capitally; buys Pete's clothes, pays for his bed and supper, and puts pennies in the savings-bank. There's a brave little man for you! I wanted to see him; but he is a newsboy, and sells late papers, because, though harder work, it pays better, and the coast is clear for those who do it.

The savings-bank was a great table all full of slits, each one leading to a little place below and numbered outside, so each boy knew his own. Once a month the bank is opened, and the lads take out what they like, or have it invested in a big bank for them to have when they find homes out West, as many do, and make good farmers. One boy was putting in some pennies as we looked, and I asked how much he had saved this month. "Fourteen dollars, ma'am," says the thirteen-year-older, proudly slipping in the last cent. A prize of $3 is offered to the lad who saves the most in a month.

The beds upstairs were in two immense rooms, ever so much larger than our town hall,—one hundred in one, and one hundred and eighty in another,—all narrow beds with a blue quilt, neat pillow, and clean sheet. They are built in long rows, one over another, and the upper boy has to climb up as on board ship. I'd have liked to see one hundred and eighty all in their "by-lows" at once, and I asked the man if they did n't train when all were in. "Lord, ma'am, they're up at five, poor little chaps, and are so tired at night that they drop off right away. Now and then some boy kicks up a little row, but we have a watchman, and he soon settles 'em."

He also told me how that very day a neat, smart young man came in, and said he was one of their boys who went West with a farmer only a little while ago; and now he owned eighty acres of land, had a good house, and was doing well, and had come to New York to find his sister, and to take her away to live with him. Was n't that nice? Lots of boys do as well. Instead of loafing round the streets and getting into mischief, they are taught to be tidy, industrious, and honest, and then sent away into the wholesome country to support themselves.

It was funny to see 'em scrub in the bath-room,— feet and faces,—comb their hair, fold up their old clothes in the dear cubbies, which make them so happy because they feel that they *own* something.

The man said every boy wanted one, even though he had neither shoes nor jacket to put in it; but would lay away an old rag of a cap or a dirty tippet with an air of satisfaction fine to see. Some lads sat reading, and the man said they loved it so they 'd read all night, if allowed. At nine he gave the word, "Bed!" and away went the lads, trooping up to sleep in shirts and trousers, as nightgowns are not provided. How would a boy I know like that,—a boy who likes to have "trommin" on his nighties? Of course, I don't mean dandy Don! Oh, dear no!

After nine [if late in coming in] they are fined five cents; after ten, ten cents; and after eleven they can't come in at all. This makes them steady, keeps them out of harm, and gives them time for study. Some go to the theatre, and sleep anywhere; some sleep at the Home, but go out for a better breakfast than they get there, as the swell ones are fond of goodies, and live well in their funny way. Coffee and cakes at Fulton Market is "the tip-top grub," and they often spend all their day's earnings in a play and a supper, and sleep in boxes or cellars after it.

Lots of pussies were round the kitchen; and one black one I called a bootblack, and a gray kit that yowled loud was a newsboy. That made some chaps laugh, and they nodded at me as I went out. Nice boys! but I know some nicer ones. Write and tell me something about my poor Squabby.

By-by, your

WEEDY.

Jacob Riis
(1849–1914)

Jacob Riis was a Danish American journalist, social reformer and photographer now best remembered for his pioneering flash-photography work and the series of essays he would write on the crushing overcrowding, heart-wrenching poverty and catastrophic infant mortality rates that were unfolding in the tenements of the Lower East Side at the turn of the twentieth century. Riis's still most prominent work, the landmark 1890 exposé *How the Other Half Lives*, near single-handedly helped to bring some of New York City's most pressing social problems to the forefront of public consciousness and swayed leading politicians, including Theodore Roosevelt, to pledge to ameliorate much of what Riis captured through his words and images. The vantage point that Riis brought to the crushing conditions he aimed to change was deeply shaped by the precarity he had himself experienced when he immigrated to the city in 1870 at the age of just twenty-one; memories he returned to in detail in his 1901 autobiography, *The Making of an American*. In this extract, Riis makes a powerful case for the way that appalling living conditions have become an incubator of crime and misery in America's great metropolis.

from How the Other Half Lives

Long ago it was said that "one half of the world does not know how the other half lives." That was true then. It did not know because it did not care. The half that was on top cared little for the struggles, and less for the fate of those who were underneath, so long as it was able to hold them there and keep its own seat. There came a time when the discomfort and crowding below were so great, and the consequent upheavals so violent, that it was no longer an easy thing to do, and then the upper half fell to inquiring what was the matter. Information on the subject has been accumulating rapidly since, and the whole world has had its hands full answering for its old ignorance.

In New York, the youngest of the world's great cities, that time came later than elsewhere, because the crowding had not been so great. There were those who believed that it would never come; but their hopes were vain. Greed and reckless selfishness wrought like results here as in the cities of older lands. "When the great riot occurred in 1863," so reads the testimony of the Secretary of the Prison Association of New York before a legislative committee appointed to investigate causes of the increase of crime in the State twenty-five years ago, "every hiding-place and nursery of crime discovered itself by immediate and active participation in the operations of the mob. Those very places and domiciles, and all that are like them, are to-day nurseries of crime, and of the vices and disorderly courses which lead to crime. By far the largest part—eighty per cent. at least—of crimes against property and against the person are perpetrated by individuals who have either lost connection with home life, or never had any, or whose *homes had ceased to be sufficiently separate, decent, and desirable to afford what are regarded as ordinary wholesome influences of home and family.* . . . The younger criminals seem to come almost exclusively from the worst tenement house districts, that is, when traced back to the very places where they had their homes in the city here." Of one thing New York made sure at that early stage of the inquiry: the boundary line of the Other Half lies through the tenements.

It is ten years and over, now, since that line divided New York's population evenly. To-day three-fourths of its people live in the tenements, and the nineteenth century drift of the population to the cities is sending ever-increasing multitudes to crowd them. The fifteen thousand tenant houses that were the despair of the sanitarian in the past generation have swelled into thirty-seven thousand, and more than twelve hundred thousand persons call them home. The one way out he saw—rapid transit to the suburbs—has brought no relief. We know now that there is no way out; that the "system" that was the evil offspring of public neglect and private greed has come to stay, a storm-centre forever of our civilization. Nothing is left but to make the best of a bad bargain.

What the tenements are and how they grew to what they are, we shall see hereafter. The story is dark enough, drawn from the plain public records, to send a chill to any heart. If it shall appear that the sufferings and the sins of the "other half," and the evil they breed, are but as a just punishment upon the community that gave it no other choice, it will be because that is the truth. The boundary line lies there because, while the forces for good on one side vastly outweigh the bad—it were not well otherwise—in the tenements all the influences make for evil; because they are the hot-beds of the epidemics that carry death to rich and poor alike; the nurseries of pauperism and crime that fill our jails and police courts; that throw off a scum of forty thousand human wrecks to the island asylums and workhouses year by year; that turned out in the last eight years a round half million beggars to prey upon our charities; that maintain a standing army of ten thousand tramps with all that that implies; because, above all, they touch the family life with deadly moral contagion. This is their worst crime, inseparable from the system. That we have to own it the child of our own wrong does not excuse it, even though it gives it claim upon our utmost patience and tenderest charity.

What are you going to do about it? is the question of to-day. It was asked once of our city in taunting defiance by a band of political cutthroats, the legitimate outgrowth of life on the tenement-house level. Law and order found the answer then and prevailed. With our enormously swelling population held in this galling bondage, will that answer always be given? It will depend on how fully the situation that prompted the challenge is grasped.

Stephen Crane
(1871–1900)

Stephen Crane was an extraordinarily talented realist writer who achieved considerable acclaim from prominent American writers and then meteoric international fame in the decade preceding his death from tuberculosis aged twenty-eight. Born in Newark, New Jersey to a devout Methodist family – his father was a minister, and his mother regularly published articles in religious periodicals on a variety of social issues – Crane would carry their abiding interest in social problems with him when he moved to New York at the age of twenty to begin working as a freelance reporter for the *New York Tribune*. But he would also actively work to jettison that past, embracing a non-traditional life in the bohemian underbelly of the city and making that world central to many of his writings, including his 1893 novella, *Maggie: A Girl of the Streets*, a tale of urban slum life shocking enough to the sensibilities of turn-of-the-century readers to require him to adopt a pseudonym. In this selection from *Maggie*, Crane offers readers a vivid and harrowing glimpse of childhood in the slums of New York.

from Maggie: A Girl of the Streets

Eventually they entered a dark region where, from a careening building, a dozen gruesome doorways gave up loads of babies to the street and the gutter. A wind of early autumn raised yellow dust from cobbles and swirled it against a hundred windows. Long streamers of garments fluttered from fire-escapes. In all unhandy places there were buckets, brooms, rags, and bottles. In the street infants played or fought with other infants or sat stupidly in the way of vehicles. Formidable women, with uncombed hair and disordered dress, gossipped while leaning on railings, or screamed in frantic quarrels. Withered persons, in curious postures of submission to something, sat smoking pipes in obscure corners. A thousand odours of cooking food came forth to the street. The building quivered and creaked from the weight of humanity stamping about in its bowels.

A small ragged girl dragged a red, bawling infant along the crowded ways. He was hanging back, baby-like, bracing his wrinkled, bare legs.

The little girl cried out: "Ah, Tommie, come ahn. Dere's Jimmie and fader. Don't be a-pullin' me back."

She jerked the baby's arm impatiently. He fell on his face, roaring. With a second jerk she pulled him to his feet, and they went on. With the obstinacy of his order, he protested against being dragged in a chosen direction. He made heroic endeavours to keep on his legs, denounced his sister, and consumed a bit of orange peeling which he chewed between the times of his infantile orations.

As the sullen-eyed man, followed by the blood-covered boy, drew near, the little girl burst into reproachful cries. "Ah, Jimmie, youse bin fightin' agin."

The urchin swelled disdainfully.

"Ah, what d' h—l, Mag. See?"

The little girl upbraided him. "Youse allus fightin', Jimmie, an' yeh knows it puts mudder out when yehs come home half dead, an' it's like we'll all get a poundin'."

She began to weep. The babe threw back his head and roared at his prospects.

"Ah," cried Jimmie, "shut up er I'll smack yer mout'. See?"

As his sister continued her lamentations, he suddenly struck her. The little girl reeled and, recovering herself, burst into tears and quaveringly cursed him. As she slowly retreated, her brother advanced dealing her cuffs. The father heard and turned about.

"Stop that, Jim, d'yeh hear? Leave yer sister alone on the street. It's like I can never beat any sense into yer wooden head."

The urchin raised his voice in defiance to his parent and continued his attacks. The babe bawled tremendously, protesting with great violence. During his sister's hasty manœuvres he was dragged by the arm.

Finally the procession plunged into one of the

gruesome doorways. They crawled up dark stairways and along cold, gloomy halls. At last the father pushed open a door and they entered a lighted room in which a large woman was rampant.

She stopped in a career from a seething stove to a pan-covered table. As the father and children filed in she peered at them.

"Eh, what? Been fightin' agin!" She threw herself upon Jimmie. The urchin tried to dart behind the others, and in the scuffle the babe, Tommie, was knocked down. He protested with his usual vehemence, because they had bruised his tender shins against a table leg.

The mother's massive shoulders heaved with anger. Grasping the urchin by the neck and shoulder she shook him until he rattled. She dragged him to an unholy sink, and, soaking a rag in water, began to scrub his lacerated face with it. Jimmie screamed in pain and tried to twist his shoulders out of the clasp of the huge arms.

The babe sat on the floor watching the scene, his face in contortions like that of a woman at a tragedy. The father, with a newly ladened pipe in his mouth, sat in a backless chair near the stove. Jimmie's cries annoyed him. He turned about and bellowed at his wife:

"Let the kid alone for a minute, will yeh, Mary? Yer allus poundin' 'im. When I come nights I can't git no rest 'cause yer allus poundin' a kid. Let up, d'yeh hear? Don't be allus poundin' a kid."

The woman's operations on the urchin instantly

increased in violence. At last she tossed him to a corner where he limply lay weeping.

The wife put her immense hands on her hips, and with a chieftainlike stride approached her husband.

"Ho!" she said, with a great grunt of contempt. "An' what in the devil are you stickin' your nose for?"

The babe crawled under the table and, turning, peered out cautiously. The ragged girl retreated, and the urchin in the corner drew his legs carefully beneath him.

The man puffed his pipe calmly and put his great muddied boots on the back part of the stove.

"Go t' h—l," he said tranquilly.

The woman screamed and shook her fists before her husband's eyes. The rough yellow of her face and neck flared suddenly crimson. She began to howl.

He puffed imperturbably at his pipe for a time, but finally arose and went to look out of the window into the darkening chaos of back yards.

"You've been drinkin', Mary," he said. "You'd better let up on the bot', ol' woman, or you'll git done."

"You're a liar. I ain't had a drop," she roared in reply. They had a lurid altercation.

The babe was staring out from under the table, his small face working in his excitement. The ragged girl went stealthily over to the corner where the urchin lay.

"Are yehs hurted much, Jimmie?" she whispered timidly.

"Not a little bit. See?" growled the little boy.

"Will I wash d' blood?"

"Naw!"

"Will I——"

"When I catch dat Riley kid I'll break 'is face! Dat's right! See?"

He turned his face to the wall as if resolved grimly to bide his time.

In the quarrel between husband and wife the woman was victor. The man seized his hat and rushed from the room, apparently determined upon a vengeful drunk. She followed to the door and thundered at him as he made his way downstairs.

She returned and stirred up the room until her children were bobbing about like bubbles.

"Git outa d' way," she bawled persistently, waving feet with their dishevelled shoes near the heads of her children. She shrouded herself, puffing and snorting, in a cloud of steam at the stove, and eventually extracted a frying pan full of potatoes that hissed.

She flourished it. "Come t' yer suppers, now," she cried with sudden exasperation. "Hurry up, now, er I'll help yeh!"

The children scrambled hastily. With prodigious clatter they arranged themselves at table. The babe sat with his feet dangling high from a precarious infant's chair and gorged his small stomach. Jimmie forced, with feverish rapidity, the grease-enveloped pieces between his wounded lips. Maggie, with side glances of fear of interruption, ate like a small pursued tigress.

The mother sat blinking at them. She delivered reproaches, swallowed potatoes, and drank from a yellow-brown bottle. After a time her mood changed and she wept as she carried little Tommie into another room and laid him to sleep, with his fists doubled, in an old quilt of faded red and green grandeur. Then she came and moaned by the stove. She rocked to and fro upon a chair, shedding tears and crooning miserably to the two children about their "poor mother" and "yer fader, d—n 'is soul."

The little girl plodded between the table and the chair with a dish pan on it. She tottered on her small legs beneath burdens of dishes.

Jimmie sat nursing his various wounds. He cast furtive glances at his mother. His practised eye perceived her gradually emerge from a mist of muddled sentiment until her brain burned in drunken heat. He sat breathless.

Maggie broke a plate.

The mother started to her feet as if propelled.

"Good Gawd!" she howled. Her glittering eyes fastened on her child with sudden hatred. The fervent red of her face turned almost to purple. The little boy ran to the halls, shrieking like a monk in an earthquake.

He floundered about in darkness until he found the stairs. He stumbled, panic-stricken, to the next floor. An old woman opened a door. A light behind her threw a flare on the urchin's face.

"Eh, child, what is it dis time? Is yer fader beatin' yer mudder, or yer mudder beatin' yer fader?"

Abraham Cahan
(1860–1951)

Born in Lithuania, pioneering Jewish American writer, journalist and editor Abraham Cahan moved to New York in 1882 at the age of twenty-one. Cahan would spend his first six years in the city working in a cigar factory, teaching himself English and immersing himself in the Lower East Side's vibrant Yiddish Socialist movement. He is now best remembered for the groundbreaking novels and short stories that he authored in English about the lives of Jewish immigrants in New York, including his debut novel, *Yekl: A Tale of the New York Ghetto* (1896), and *The Rise of David Levinsky* (1917), at the encouragement of W. D. Howells. But he made an equally lasting mark through his work as a journalist, and the four decades he spent editing *The Forward*, the most influential Yiddish Socialist newspaper in America which, at its peak, reached nearly a quarter of a million readers daily. This extract from his debut novel offers readers a taste of the sights and sounds that newly arrived Jewish immigrants encountered as they crowded into the Yiddish quarter of New York, and a searing sense of the political repression that had spurred on so many of them to emigrate.

from Yekl: A Tale of the New York Ghetto

It was after seven in the evening when Jake finished his last jacket. Some of the operators had laid down their work before, while others cast an envious glance on him as he was dressing to leave, and fell to their machines with reluctantly redoubled energy. Fanny was a week worker and her time had been up at seven; but on this occasion her toilet had taken an uncommonly long time, and she was not ready until Jake got up from his chair. Then she left the room rather suddenly and with a demonstrative "Good-night all!"

When Jake reached the street he found her on the sidewalk, making a pretense of brushing one of her sleeves with the cuff of the other.

"So kvick?" she asked, raising her head in feigned surprise.

"You cull dot kvick?" he returned grimly. "Good-bye!"

"Say, ain't you goin' to dance to-night, really?" she queried shamefacedly.

"I tol' you I vouldn't."

"What does *she* want of me?" he complained to himself proceeding on his way. He grew conscious of his low spirits, and, tracing them with some effort to their source, he became gloomier still. "No more fun for me!" he decided. "I shall get them over here and begin a new life."

After supper, which he had taken, as usual, at his lodgings, he went out for a walk. He was firmly determined to keep himself from visiting Joe Peltner's dancing academy, and accordingly he took a direction opposite to Suffolk Street, where that establishment was situated. Having passed a few blocks, however, his feet, contrary to his will, turned into a side street and thence into one leading to Suffolk. "I shall only drop in to tell Joe that I can not sell any of his ball tickets, and return them," he attempted to deceive his own conscience. Hailing this pretext with delight he quickened his pace as much as the overcrowded sidewalks would allow.

He had to pick and nudge his way through dense swarms of bedraggled half-naked humanity; past garbage barrels rearing their overflowing contents in sickening piles, and lining the streets in malicious suggestion of rows of trees; underneath tiers and tiers of fire escapes, barricaded and festooned with mattresses, pillows, and featherbeds not yet gathered in for the night. The pent-in sultry atmosphere was laden with nausea and pierced with a discordant and, as it were, plaintive buzz. Supper had been despatched in a hurry, and the teeming populations of the cyclopic tenement houses were out in full force "for fresh air," as even these people will say in mental quotation marks.

Suffolk Street is in the very thick of the battle for breath. For it lies in the heart of that part of the East Side which has within the last two or three decades become the Ghetto of the American metropolis, and, indeed, the metropolis of the Ghettos of the world. It is one of the most densely populated spots on the face of the earth—a seething human sea fed by streams, streamlets, and rills of immigration flowing from all the Yiddish-speaking centres of Europe. Hardly a block but shelters Jews from every nook and corner of Russia, Poland, Galicia, Hungary, Roumania; Lithuanian Jews, Volhynian Jews, south Russian Jews, Bessarabian Jews; Jews crowded out of the "pale of Jewish settlement"; Russified Jews expelled from Moscow, St. Petersburg, Kieff, or Saratoff; Jewish runaways from justice; Jewish refugees from crying political and economical injustice; people torn from a hard-gained foothold in life and from deep-rooted attachments by the caprice of intolerance or the wiles of demagoguery—innocent scapegoats of a guilty Government for its outraged populace to misspend its blind fury upon; students shut out of the Russian universities, and come to these shores in quest of learning; artisans, merchants, teachers, rabbis, artists, beggars—all come in search of fortune. Nor is there a tenement house but harbours in its bosom specimens of all the whimsical metamorphoses wrought upon the children of Israel of the great modern exodus by the vicissitudes of life in this their Promised Land of to-day. You find there Jews born to plenty, whom the new conditions have delivered up to the clutches of penury; Jews reared in the straits of need, who have here risen to prosperity; good people morally degraded in the struggle for success amid an unwonted environment; moral outcasts lifted from the mire, purified, and imbued with self-respect; educated men and women with their intellectual polish tarnished in the inclement weather of adversity; ignorant sons of toil grown enlightened—in fine, people with all sorts of antecedents, tastes, habits, inclinations, and speaking all sorts of subdialects of the same jargon, thrown pellmell into one social caldron—a human hodgepodge with its component parts changed but not yet fused into one homogeneous whole.

And so the "stoops," sidewalks, and pavements of Suffolk Street were thronged with panting, chattering, or frisking multitudes. In one spot the scene received a kind of weird picturesqueness from children dancing on the pavement to the strident music hurled out into the tumultuous din from a row of the open and brightly illuminated windows of what appeared to be a new tenement house. Some of the young women on the sidewalk opposite raised a longing eye to these windows, for floating by through the dazzling light within were young women like themselves with masculine arms round their waists.

Maxim Gorky
(1868–1936)

Maxim Gorky was an influential Russian writer and biting social critic who won international acclaim – and five nominations for the Nobel Prize in Literature – for his short stories, novels, plays and autobiographical trilogy. First as a journalist and later in his fiction, Gorky cast an unrelenting gaze on the most pressing social ills of his day, winning him the admiration of Russian writers such as Tolstoy but also the ire of the Russian government, eventually forcing him into exile. New York was the first stop on Gorky's much-anticipated US lecture tour in 1906 following his release from prison in Russia. Although he would later describe the city as 'a monstrous metropolis', he was warmly welcomed by New York's socialist, anarchist and literary circles. But, when the US press revealed the scandal that he was travelling with his long-time lover rather than his wife, he was forced to cut short his visit. This selection, from an essay first published in the influential American magazine the *Independent*, meditates on his visit to Coney Island, hauntingly capturing at once the extraordinary beauty he finds in New York's 'dreamland' and so too its monstrous emptiness.

from Boredom

With the advent of night a fantastic city all of fire suddenly rises from the ocean into the sky. Thousands of ruddy sparks glimmer in the darkness, limning in fine, sensitive outline on the black background of the sky, shapely towers of miraculous castles, palaces and temples. Golden gossamer threads tremble in the air. They intertwine in transparent, flaming patterns, which flutter and melt away in love with their own beauty mirrored in the waters. Fabulous and beyond conceiving, ineffably beautiful, is this fiery scintillation. It burns but does not consume. Its palpitations are scarce visible. In the wilderness of sky and ocean rises the magic picture of a flaming city. Over it quiver the reddened heavens, and below the water reflects its contours, blending them into a whimsical blotch of molten gold.

Strange thoughts fill the mind at the sight of this play of fire. In the halls of the palaces, in the radiant gleam of flaming mirth, methinks, strains of music float, soft and proud, such as mortal ear has never heard. On the melodious current of their sounds the best thoughts of the world are carried along like sailing stars. The stars meet in a sacred dance, they throw out dazzling sparks, and as they clasp in a momentary embrace, they give birth to new flames, new thoughts.

I see a huge cradle, marvelously wrought of golden

tissue, flowers and stars rocking yonder in the soft darkness, upon the trembling bosom of the ocean.

There at night rests the sun.

But the sun of the day brings man nearer to the truth of life. Then the fiery magic castles are tall white buildings.

The blue mist of the ocean vapors mingles with the drab smoke of the metropolis across the harbor. Its flimsy white structures are enveloped in a transparent sheet, in which they quiver like a mirage. They seem to beckon alluringly, and offer quiet and beauty.

The city hums with its constant, insatiate, hungry roar. The strained sound, agitating the air and the soul, the ceaseless bellow of iron, the melancholy wail of life driven by the power of gold, the cold, cynical whistle of the Yellow Devil scare the people away from the turmoil of the earth burdened and besmirched by the ill-smelling body of the city. And the people go forth to the shore of the sea, where the beautiful white buildings stand and promise respite and tranquillity.

The buildings huddle close together on a long, sandy strip of land, which, like a sharp knife, plunges deep into the dark water. The sand glitters in the sun with a warm, yellow gleam, and the transparent buildings stand out on its velvety expanse like thin white silk embroidery. The effect is as of rich garments thrown carelessly on the bosom of the island by some bather before plunging into the waters.

I turn my gaze wistfully upon this island. I long to

nestle in its downy texture. I would recline on its luxurious folds, and from there look out into the wide spaces, where white birds dart swiftly and noiselessly, where ocean and sky lie drowsing in the scorching gleam of the sun.

This is Coney Island.

On Monday the metropolitan newspapers triumphantly announce:

"Three Hundred Thousand People in Coney Island Yesterday. Twenty-three Children Lost."

"There's something doing there" the reader thinks.

First a long ride by trolley thru Brooklyn and Long Island amid the dust and noise of the streets. Then the gaze is met by the sight of dazzling, magnificent Coney Island. From the very first moment of arrival at this city of fire, the eye is blinded. It is assailed by thousands of cold, white sparks, and for a long time can distinguish nothing in the scintillating dust round about. Everything whirls and dazzles, and blends into a tempestuous ferment of fiery foam. The visitor is stunned; his consciousness is withered by the intense gleam; his thoughts are routed from his mind; he becomes a particle in the crowd. People wander about in the flashing, blinding fire intoxicated and devoid of will. A dull-white mist penetrates their brains, greedy expectation envelopes their souls. Dazed by the brilliancy the throngs wind about like dark bands in the surging sea of light, pressed upon all sides by the black bournes of night.

Everywhere electric bulbs shed their cold, garish gleam. They shine on posts and walls, on window casings and cornices: they stretch in an even line along the high tubes of the power-house; they burn on all the roofs, and prick the eye with the sharp needles of their dead, indifferent sparkle. The people screw up their eyes, and smiling disconcertedly crawl along the ground like the heavy line of a tangled chain.

A man must make a great effort not to lose himself in the crowd, not to be overwhelmed by his amazement—an amazement in which there is neither transport nor joy. But if he succeeds in individualizing himself, he finds that these millions of fires produce a dismal, all-revealing light. Tho they hint at the possibility of beauty, they everywhere discover a dull, gloomy ugliness. The city, magic and fantastic from afar, now appears an absurd jumble of straight lines of wood, a cheap, hastily constructed toy-house for the amusement of children. Dozens of white buildings, monstrously diverse, not one with even the suggestion of beauty. They are built of wood, and smeared over with peeling white paint, which gives them the appearance of suffering with the same skin disease. The high turrets and low colonnades extend in two dead-even lines insipidly pressing upon each other. Everything is stripped naked by the dispassionate glare. The glare is everywhere, and nowhere a shadow. Each building stands there like a dumbfounded fool with wide-open mouth, and sends forth the glare of brass trumpets and the whining rumble of orchestrions. Inside is a cloud of smoke and the dark figures of the people. The people eat, drink and smoke.

But no human voice is heard. The monotonous hissing of the arc lights fills the air, the sounds of music, the cheap notes of the orchestrions, and the thin, continuous sputtering of the sausage-frying counters. All these sounds mingle in an importunate hum, as of some thick, taut chord. And if the human voice breaks into this ceaseless resonance, it is like a frightened whisper. Everything round about glitters insolently and reveals its own dismal ugliness.

The soul is seized with a desire for a living, beautiful fire, a sublime fire, which should free the people from the slavery of a varied boredom. For this boredom deafens their ears and blinds their eyes. The soul would burn away all this allurement, all this mad frenzy, this dead magnificence and spiritual penury. It would have a merry dancing and shouting and singing: it would see a passionate play of the motley tongues of fire; it would have joyousness and life.

THE POETRY OF THE CITY

WALT WHITMAN
(1819–1892)

Born on Long Island and raised in Brooklyn, Walt Whitman would become one of America's most influential poets. Among his many admirers outside the US were working-class readers in Bolton and the Nobel Prize-winning Chilean poet Pablo Neruda. Whitman got his start as a writer working first as a printer and later as a journalist and editor. In 1855, while living at 99 Ryerson Street in Brooklyn, he published the first edition of *Leaves of Grass*, a slender, self-financed volume of ecstatic free verse that celebrated the self, the body and urban life, and which grew across successive editions into one of the foundational works of American literature. His journalism similarly reflected his fascination with the rapidly growing metropolis around him. Whitman's lifelong ties to New York shaped his poetry profoundly: the East River ferry inspired 'Crossing Brooklyn Ferry', and the sounds, sights and feel of the city texture much of his verse. In this poem, first published in 1860 in the third edition of *Leaves of Grass*, the speaker goes in search of 'a word, liquid, sane, unruly, musical, self-sufficient' for his much-loved city.

Mannahatta

I was asking for something specific and perfect for my city, and behold! here is the aboriginal name!

Now I see what there is in a name, a word, liquid, sane, unruly, musical, self-sufficient,

I see that the word of my city, is that word up there,

Because I see that word nested in nests of water-bays, superb, with tall and wonderful spires,

Rich, hemmed thick all around with sailships and steamships—an island sixteen miles long, solid-founded,

Numberless crowded streets—high growths of iron, slender, strong, light, splendidly uprising toward clear skies;

Tides swift and ample, well-loved by me, toward sundown,

The flowing sea-currents, the little islands, the larger adjoining islands, the heights, the villas,

The countless masts, the white shore-steamers, the lighters, the ferry-boats, the black sea-steamers, well-model'd;

The down-town streets, the jobbers' houses of business—the houses of business of the ship-merchants, and money-brokers—the river-streets,

Immigrants arriving, fifteen or twenty thousand in a week,

The carts hauling goods—the manly race of drivers of horses—the brown-faced sailors,

The summer-air, the bright sun shining, and the sailing clouds aloft,

The winter snows, the sleigh-bells—the broken ice in the river, passing along, up or down, with the flood-tide or ebb-tide;

The mechanics of the city, the masters, well-formed, beautiful-faced, looking you straight in the eyes;

Trottoirs thronged—vehicles—Broadway—the women—the shops and shows,

The parades, processions, bugles playing, flags flying, drums beating;

A million people—manners free and superb—open voices—hospitality—the most courageous and friendly young men;

The free city! no slaves! no owners of slaves!

The beautiful city! the city of hurried and sparkling waters! the city of spires and masts!

The city nested in bays! my city!

The city of such women, I am mad to be with them! I will return after death to be with them!

The city of such young men, I swear I cannot live happy, without I often go talk, walk, eat, drink, sleep, with them!

Emma Lazarus
(1849–1887)

Born into a prominent Sephardic Jewish family in New York City, Emma Lazarus was a pioneering poet and essayist who devoted her short but influential literary career to exploring Jewish American identity and pressing social justice issues, particularly the plight of refugees fleeing antisemitism in Europe. While now best remembered for poetry collections such as *Admetus and Other Poems* (1871) and *Songs of a Semite* (1882), Lazarus also published the novel *Alide* (1874), the play *The Spagnoletto* (1876) and a translation of Heinriche Heine's poetry and ballads. Moved by the arrival of Jewish refugees fleeing Russian pogroms, she volunteered at immigrant aid stations at Castle Garden and Ward's Island, experiences that profoundly sharpened both her political commitment and her poetic vision. The poem included here, 'The New Colossus', is by far her most famous work, written for an exhibition raising funds for the pedestal of the Statue of Liberty. The sonnet's hopeful – and pointedly insistent – welcome to the 'huddled masses yearning to breathe free' was famously later inscribed as a plaque mounted inside the pedestal in 1903, helping to cement New York's identity as the great gateway for those arriving in the US.

The New Colossus

Not like the brazen giant of Greek fame,
With conquering limbs astride from land to land;
Here at our sea-washed, sunset gates shall stand
A mighty woman with a torch, whose flame
Is the imprisoned lightning, and her name
Mother of Exiles. From her beacon-hand
Glows world-wide welcome; her mild eyes command
The air-bridged harbor that twin cities frame.
"Keep, ancient lands, your storied pomp!" cries she
With silent lips. "Give me your tired, your poor,
Your huddled masses yearning to breathe free,
The wretched refuse of your teeming shore.
Send these, the homeless, tempest-tost to me,
I lift my lamp beside the golden door!"

SARA TEASDALE
(1884–1933)

Born in St Louis, Missouri, Sara Teasdale was one of the most popular lyric poets of the early twentieth century. In a sense, she is very much a Midwestern poet: she first published her work in *The Potter's Wheel*, a monthly hand-printed journal she started as a teenager with young women friends in St Louis; her debut collection, *Sonnets to Duse and Other Poems* (1907), was first published in Chicago; and her work found early support from Harriet Monroe, founder of *Poetry Magazine*, likewise based there. Yet many of Teasdale's best-known lines were written in or about New York. She first visited the city at twenty-six, when she was inducted into the Poetry Society of America. Several visits followed over the next few years, including one memorable evening spent wandering Greenwich Village in conversation with journalist John Reed, before she moved permanently to New York in 1916, where she lived for the rest of her life. The two poems here, 'Broadway' and 'The Lights of New York', were first published in her 1915 collection *Rivers to the Sea*, and both pay tribute to the 'liquid splendor' that comes to life at night in New York's wondrously electrified (and electrifying) streets.

Broadway

This is the quiet hour; the theaters
   Have gathered in their crowds, and steadily
   The million lights blaze on for few to see,
Robbing the sky of stars that should be hers.
A woman waits with bag and shabby furs,
   A somber man drifts by, and only we
   Pass up the street unwearied, warm and free,
For over us the olden magic stirs.
Beneath the liquid splendor of the lights
   We live a little ere the charm is spent;
This night is ours, of all the golden nights,
   The pavement an enchanted palace floor,
And Youth the player on the viol, who sent
   A strain of music thru an open door.

The Lights of New York

The lightning spun your garment for the night
   Of silver filaments with fire shot thru,
   A broidery of lamps that lit for you
The steadfast splendor of enduring light.
The moon drifts dimly in the heaven's height,
   Watching with wonder how the earth she knew
   That lay so long wrapped deep in dark and dew,
Should wear upon her breast a star so white.
The festivals of Babylon were dark
   With flaring flambeaux that the wind blew down;
The Saturnalia were a wild boy's lark
   With rain-quenched torches dripping thru the town—
But you have found a god and filched from him
A fire that neither wind nor rain can dim.

Edna St Vincent Millay
(1892–1950)

Now best remembered for her masterful blending of traditional forms and modernist sensibilities, her daring explorations of desire and her outspoken progressive views, Edna St Vincent Millay was one of the most celebrated American poets of her generation. Born in Maine, she published her poetry from a very young age in prominent children's magazines and rose to fame at the age of twenty after her poem 'Renascence' won wide acclaim in 1912. After graduating from Vassar in 1917, she moved to New York City, where she quickly became a central figure in Greenwich Village's bohemian scene, performing in socialist plays and giving spellbinding readings of her poetry in various cafes and bookstores in the Village. She lived at 75½ Bedford Street, the narrowest house in Manhattan, from 1923 to 1925. Millay's collections *A Few Figs from Thistles* (1920) and *The Harp-Weaver and Other Poems* (1922), the latter of which contained the poem for which she won the Pulitzer Prize in 1923, helped cement her reputation as both a serious poet and a popular icon of the Jazz Age, and she also wrote a number of experimental plays. New York – as sights, sounds, tastes, subway ticket stubs and ferry rides – is evoked in gorgeous detail in her poem 'Recuerdo', which was first published in 1919.

Recuerdo

We were very tired, we were very merry—
We had gone back and forth all night on the ferry.
It was bare and bright, and smelled like a stable—
But we looked into a fire, we leaned across a table,
We lay on the hill-top underneath the moon;
And the whistles kept blowing, and the dawn came soon.

We were very tired, we were very merry—
We had gone back and forth all night on the ferry;
And you ate an apple, and I ate a pear,
From a dozen of each we had bought somewhere;
And the sky went wan, and the wind came cold,
And the sun rose dripping, a bucketful of gold.

We were very tired, we were very merry,
We had gone back and forth all night on the ferry.
We hailed, "Good morrow, mother!" to a shawl-covered head,
And bought a morning paper, which neither of us read;
And she wept, "God bless you!" for the apples and the pears,
And we gave her all our money but our subway fares.

Claude McKay
(1890–1948)

Claude McKay was an influential Jamaican American poet and novelist, a pioneering queer writer and one of the central figures of the Harlem Renaissance. His early poetry turned its attention to the sounds of peasant life in Jamaica, but he moved to New York in 1914 aged twenty-four after finishing his studies. The city's racial tensions and cultural life deeply shaped his work, on full display in his militant 1919 sonnet 'If We Must Die', written in response to that year's wave of racist violence. His collection *Harlem Shadows* (1922) was among the first major works of the Harlem Renaissance, while his novel *Home to Harlem* (1928) offered an unflinching portrait of Black urban life and became a huge bestseller. Later novels such as *Banjo* (1929) and *Banana Bottom* (1933) extended his exploration of Black diasporic life and identity. Although McKay spent extended periods in London, Paris, Moscow and Tangier, Harlem remained his spiritual home. In the two poems included here, 'The Tropics in New York' and 'On Broadway', McKay interweaves the tastes and colours of the Caribbean and New York, and captures the crowds and 'bright fantastic glow' of one of New York's most enduringly famous streets.

The Tropics in New York

Bananas ripe and green, and ginger-root,
    Cocoa in pods and alligator pears,
And tangerines and mangoes and grape fruit,
    Fit for the highest prize at parish fairs,

Set in the window, bringing memories
    Of fruit-trees laden by low-singing rills,
And dewy dawns, and mystical blue skies
    In benediction over nun-like hills.

My eyes grew dim, and I could no more gaze;
    A wave of longing through my body swept,
And, hungry for the old, familiar ways,
    I turned aside and bowed my head and wept.

On Broadway

About me young and careless feet
Linger along the garish street;
   Above, a hundred shouting signs
Shed down their bright fantastic glow
   Upon the merry crowd and lines
Of moving carriages below.
Oh wonderful is Broadway—only
My heart, my heart is lonely.

Desire naked, linked with Passion,
Goes strutting by in brazen fashion;
   From playhouse, cabaret and inn
The rainbow lights of Broadway blaze
   All gay without, all glad within;
As in a dream I stand and gaze
At Broadway, shining Broadway—only
My heart, my heart is lonely.

Langston Hughes
(1901–1967)

Langston Hughes was the pre-eminent poet of the Harlem Renaissance and a titanic figure in twentieth-century American literature. Born in Joplin, Missouri, he came to New York as a young man to study at Columbia University, but it was the community of writers and artists that he found in Harlem that most shaped his career. Hughes's first collection, *The Weary Blues* (1926), captured the rhythms of jazz and blues and announced a new Black aesthetic grounded in the sounds and experiences of everyday working-class, African American life. Over the next four decades, he produced poems, essays, plays, short stories and two memoirs. Although he travelled widely – covering the Spanish Civil War for the *Baltimore African American* and making visits to Cuba, Haiti, Japan and the Soviet Union in the 1930s – he continued to draw sustenance and inspiration from Harlem's people, music and politics, and lived for twenty years in a brownstone at 20 East 127th Street, a registered landmark which is now open to the public. In 'Lenox Avenue: Midnight', first published in his 1926 collection, *The Weary Blues*, Hughes captures the rhythm and rumble of the street famously at the heart of Harlem's jazz club and arts scene.

Lenox Avenue: Midnight

The rhythm of life
Is a jazz rhythm,
Honey.
The gods are laughing at us.

The broken heart of love,
The weary, weary heart of pain,—
   Overtones,
   Undertones,
To the rumble of street cars,
To the swish of rain.

Lenox Avenue,
Honey.
Midnight,
And the gods are laughing at us.

Elizabeth Bishop
(1911–1979)

Elizabeth Bishop was an extraordinarily gifted poet who gained substantial regard during her lifetime and even greater critical recognition following her death. Born in Worcester, Massachusetts and raised in Nova Scotia, she called a number of cities home – including Key West and Rio de Janeiro – over the course of her career. No plaques commemorate the six apartments and at least seven hotels where Bishop resided in New York for long stretches during her lifetime, beginning with her first move to the city in 1934 following her graduation from Vassar. Her own feelings about New York were complex: she once confessed that she 'never liked' the city, and the death by suicide of her lover Lota de Macedo Soares in Bishop's West Village apartment at 61 Perry Street in 1967 prompted a move to Boston, where she resided until her death. But she maintained close ties to New York both through her friendships and her connections to the *New Yorker* magazine, where she published fifty poems and five short stories. In this ecstatic poem, written in 1948, Bishop implores her dear friend to 'come flying' across the ferry to meet her so they can drink in the hum (and 'soft uninvented music') of the city together.

Invitation to Miss Marianne Moore

From Brooklyn, over the Brooklyn Bridge, on this fine
   morning,
     please come flying.
In a cloud of fiery pale chemicals,
     please come flying,
to the rapid rolling of thousands of small blue drums
descending out of the mackerel sky
over the glittering grandstand of harbor-water.
     please come flying.

Whistles, pennants and smoke are blowing. The ships
are signaling cordially with multitudes of flags
rising and falling like birds all over the harbor,
Enter: two rivers, gracefully bearing
countless little pellucid jellies
in cut-glass epergnes dragging with silver chains.
The flight is safe; the weather is all arranged.
The waves are running in verses this fine morning.
     Please come flying.

Come with the pointed toe of each black shoe
trailing a sapphire highlight,
with a black capeful of butterfly wings and bon-mots,
with heaven knows how many angels all riding
on the broad black brim of your hat,
     please come flying.

Bearing a musical inaudible abacus,
a slight censorious frown, and blue ribbons,
  please come flying.
Facts and skyscrapers glint in the tide; Manhattan
is all awash with morals this fine morning.
  so please come flying.

Mounting the sky with natural heroism.
above the accidents, above the malignant movies,
the taxicabs and injustices at large,
while horns are resounding in your beautiful ears
that simultaneously listen to
a soft uninvented music, fit for the musk deer,
  please come flying.

For whom the grim museums will behave
like courteous male bower-birds,
for whom the agreeable lions lie in wait
on the steps of the Public Library,
eager to rise and follow through the doors
up into the reading rooms,
  please come flying.
We can sit down and weep; we can go shopping,
or play at a game of constantly being wrong
with a priceless set of vocabularies,
or we can bravely deplore, but please
  please come flying.

With dynasties of negative constructions
darkening and dying around you,

with grammar that suddenly turns and shines
like flocks of sandpipers flying,
  please come flying.

Come like a light in the white mackerel sky,
come like a daytime comet
with a long unnebulous train of words,
from Brooklyn, over the Brooklyn Bridge, on this fine
  morning,
  please come flying.

Allen Ginsberg
(1926–1997)

Born in Newark and raised in Paterson, New Jersey, Allen Ginsberg was one of the central figures of the Beat Generation, a poet who pushed the boundaries of form, sexuality and subject matter while giving powerful voice to a generation's dissent and disaffection. He came to New York in 1943 to study at Columbia University, where he soon met Jack Kerouac, William S. Burroughs and other writers who would define the Beat movement, whose countercultural artistic energies coalesced around the experimental readings, performances and discussions they staged together at cafes and bars in and around Greenwich Village. His breakthrough poem, *Howl* (1956), with its long, incantatory lines and frank treatment of sexuality, madness and American consumer culture, quickly became a touchstone for literary rebellion and the subject of a landmark obscenity trial. Ginsberg lived for decades in New York's East Village, keeping an apartment at 437 East 12th Street. This poem, 'My Sad Self', which Ginsburg wrote in 1958 and dedicates to fellow New York poet Frank O'Hara, takes us to the top of the RCA building for a wistful and impressionistic glimpse of *his* city – people going by in 'ant cars and little yellow taxis', the 'panorama of bridges' and past loves.

My Sad Self

To Frank O'Hara

Sometimes when my eyes are red
I go up on top of the RCA Building
   and gaze at my world, Manhattan—
      my buildings, streets I've done feats in,
         lofts, beds, coldwater flats
—on Fifth Ave below which I also bear in mind,
   its ant cars, little yellow taxis, men
      walking the size of specks of wool—
Panorama of the bridges, sunrise over Brooklyn
   machine,
   sun go down over New Jersey where I was
      born
    & Paterson where I played with ants—
my later loves on 15th Street,
   my greater loves of Lower East Side,
      my once fabulous amours in the Bronx
                faraway—
paths crossing in these hidden streets,
   my history summed up, my absences
      and ecstasies in Harlem—
—sun shining down on all I own
   in one eyeblink to the horizon
      in my last eternity—
              matter is water.

Sad,
   I take the elevator and go
      down, pondering,
and walk on the pavements staring into all man's
               plateglass, faces,
   questioning after who loves,
and stop, bemused
   in front of an automobile shopwindow
standing lost in calm thought,
     traffic moving up & down 5th Avenue blocks
       behind me
         waiting for a moment when . . .

Time to go home & cook supper & listen to
         the romantic war news on the radio.
         . . . all movement stops
& I walk in the timeless sadness of existence,
   tenderness flowing thru the buildings,
     my fingertips touching reality's face,
my own face streaked with tears in the mirror
   of some window—at dusk—
         where I have no desire—
     for bonbons—or to own the dresses or Japanese
       lampshades of intellection—

   Confused by the spectacle around me,
     Man struggling up the street
        with packages, newspapers,
            ties, beautiful suits
       toward his desire

    Man, woman, streaming over the pavements
       red lights clocking hurried watches &
           movements at the curb—

And all these streets leading
   so crosswise, honking, lengthily,
       by avenues
   stalked by high buildings or crusted into slums
       thru such halting traffic
           screaming cars and engines
so painfully to this
  countryside, this graveyard
    this stillness.
             on deathbed or mountain
   once seen
      never regained or desired
         in the mind to come
where all Manhattan that I've seen must disappear.

Audre Lorde
(1934–1992)

Born in Harlem to West Indian American parents, Audre Lorde was a path-breaking queer Black feminist poet, a lyrical and fiercely political essayist, an accomplished teacher and the co-founder, in 1980, of Kitchen Table: Women of Color Press. She published her first poem, age fifteen, in *Seventeen Magazine*, and would go on to win numerous awards. Although she would live away from her natal city at various points in her career – teaching in Jackson, Mississippi, Berlin and Jamaica – New York was a crucial part of the fabric of both her life and her writing. A graduate of Hunter College and Columbia University, she worked for a number of years as a librarian in New York public schools and later as a Professor of English and Creative Writing at Hunter College. She raised her two children with her partner, Frances Clayton, at 207 St Paul's Avenue on Staten Island. In this poem, 'A Trip on the Staten Island Ferry', which she wrote for her son Jonathan, Lorde brings to incantatory life the worlds to be spotted on the constant to and fro of this boat, urging her son (and the reader) to 'cherish this city/left you by default'.

A Trip on the Staten Island Ferry

Dear Jonno
there are pigeons who nest
on the Staten Island Ferry
and raise their young
between the moving decks
and never touch
ashore.

Every voyage is a journey.

Cherish this city
left you by default
include it in your daydreams
there are still
secrets
in the streets
even I have not discovered
who knows
if the old men
who shine shoes on the Staten Island Ferry
carry their world
in a box slung across their shoulders
if they share their lunch
with birds

flying back and forth
upon an endless journey
if they ever find their way
back home.

GRIEF AND THE CITY

DAWN POWELL
(1896–1965)

Dawn Powell was one of the sharpest satirists of twentieth-century New York. Born in Mount Gilead, Ohio, she moved to New York in 1918 at the age of twenty-two. Although Powell 'came from nowhere and was no one', as Fran Lebowitz once put it, when she settled in Greenwich Village, she quickly became friends with writers such as Ernest Hemingway and e e cummings, and lived for the rest of her life in the bohemian New York world that she both delighted in and took great pleasure in skewering. Though her early works were set in Ohio, her later novels – including *A Time to Be Born* (1942) and *The Wicked Pavilion* (1954) – centered primarily on New York, satirizing its publishing and artistic scenes, often from the vantage point of a slightly hapless newcomer to the city. In this acerbic and deeply poignant extract from the opening pages of *A Time to Be Born*, Powell immerses us in a New York on the eve of the US entry into the Second World War, a moment when everyone is anxiously following the day's reports from Europe, wishing to wake up from the nightmare and dashing into dress shops and beauty salons to steel themselves for what's to come.

from A Time to Be Born

This was no time to cry over one broken heart. It was no time to worry about Vicky Haven or indeed any other young lady crossed in love, for now the universe, nothing less, was your problem. You woke in the morning with the weight of doom on your head. You lay with eyes shut wondering why you dreaded the day; was it a debt, was it a lost love?—and then you remembered the nightmare. It was a dream, you said, nothing but a dream, and the covers were thrown aside, the dream was over, now for the day. Then, fully awake, you remembered that it was no dream. Paris was gone, London was under fire, the Atlantic was now a drop of water between the flame on one side and the waiting dynamite on the other. This was a time of waiting, of marking time till ready, of not knowing what to expect or what to want either for yourself or for the world, private triumph or failure lost in the world's failure. The longed-for letter, the telephone ringing at last, the familiar knock at the door—very well, but there was still something to await—something unknown, something fantastic, perhaps the stone statue from *Don Giovanni* marching in or the gods of the mountain. Day's duties were performed to the metronome of Extras, radio broadcasts, committee conferences on war orphans, benefits for Britain, send a telegram to your congressman, watch your neighbor for free speech, vote for Willkie or for Roosevelt and banish care from the land.

This was certainly no time for Vicky Haven to engage your thoughts, for you were concerned with great nations, with war itself. Look at the jewels, the rare pelts, the gaudy birds on elaborate hairdress, and know that the war was here; already the women had inherited the earth. The ominous smell of gunpowder was matched by a rising cloud of Schiaparelli's *Shocking*. The women were once more armed, and their happy voices sang of destruction to come. Off to the relief offices they rode in their beautiful new cars, off to knit, to sew, to take part in the charade, anything to help Lady Bertrand's cause; off they rode in the new car, the new mink, the new emerald bracelet, the new electrically treated complexion, presented by or extorted from the loving-hearted gentlemen who make both women and wars possible. Off to the front with a new permanent and enough specially blended night creams to last three months dashed the intrepid girl reporters. Unable to cope with competition on the home field, failing with the rhumbas and screen tests of peacetime, they quiver for the easy drama of the trenches; they can at least play lead in these amateur theatricals.

This was a time when the artists, the intellectuals, sat in cafés and in country homes and accused each other over their brandies or their California vintages of traitorous tendencies. This was a time for them to band together in mutual antagonism, a time to bury the professional hatchet, if possible in each other, a time to stare at their flower arrangements, children bathing, and privately to weep, "What good is it? Who cares now?" The poet, disgusted with the flight of skylarks in perfect sonnet form, declaimed the power of song against brutality and raised hollow voice in feeble proof. This was no time for beauty, for love, or private future; (this was the time for ideals and quick profits on them before the world returned to reality and the drabber opportunities.) What good for new sopranos to sing "*Vici d'arte, vice d'amore*," what good for eager young students to make their bows? There was no future; every one waited, marked time, waited. For what? On Fifth Avenue and Fifty-fifth Street hundreds waited for a man on a hotel window ledge to jump; hundreds waited with craning necks and thirsty faces as if this single person's final gesture would solve the riddle of the world. Civilization stood on a ledge, and in the tension of waiting it was a relief to have one little man jump.

JESS ROW
(1974–present)

Named one of twenty 'Best Young American Novelists' by *Granta* in 2007, Jess Row is an award-winning novelist, short story writer and literary critic, and a Clinical Professor of English and Director of the Creative Writing Track at New York University. Born in Washington DC and raised in Baltimore, cities (and the suburbs around them) have long been a key preoccupation of his work. His first story collection, *The Train to Lo Wu* (2005), was set largely in Hong Kong, where he lived after graduating from Yale, and his debut novel, *Your Face in Mine* (2014), explored racial identity and reassignment against the backdrop of Baltimore. But Row is a longtime New Yorker both by choice and by marriage, and his love for and interest in the city is on intricate display in this wrenching and beautiful extract from the titular story in *Nobody Ever Gets Lost* (2011), his second short story collection. In it, he plunges us – lyrically and unsparingly – into the multiple forms of grief and connection that followed in the aftermath of 9/11.

from Nobody Ever Gets Lost

As she leaves the toll booth and pulls toward the right lane the traffic gains momentum, and the great cables of the bridge rise up on either side, like giant wings, like Gothic arches. She thinks, *This is my cathedral.* She rolls the windows down, and hot, sticky air rushes through the car, smelling of the river. Roger, she thinks, if I had your ashes I would carry them out to the middle in a Chinese takeout container, and toss them off, just casually, over my shoulder. Roger, if you could have died the way you lived, with sarcasm, with subtlety, with the Pixies on the stereo, then it would have been all right. If it had been AIDS, if it had been *leukemia,* it would have been okay, as long as we had twenty-four hours' notice, enough time to call a few friends and chill a bottle of champagne, so we could drink it at the bitter end, like Chekhov.

If you had stopped at Starbucks.

If you had lingered on the 1 reading the paper instead of taking the 2.

If you had thought it was OK to show up at work *thirty seconds late.*

If you had stopped to talk to Rachel Abramowitz, who passed you on the platform at 7:49, your college friend, whom you hadn't seen in years, instead of saying, Sorry, I've got to rush, *give me a call,* and handing her your card.

If numbers hadn't been invented.

If God hadn't been invented.

If the word *because* hadn't been invented.

If the word *therefore* hadn't been invented,

If we understood what words meant in the first place,

Then you wouldn't have been reduced to a puff of smoke, a vague and unpleasant *smell*, not a shard, not a fleck of skin or blood, you wouldn't have been sterilized out of existence by a ten-thousand-degree fire, and I wouldn't be flying across this bridge with my mouth open, as if I could eat the air. She turns her head, now halfway across, and looks down the whole length of the island, through the gray-gold haze, searching for the gap. How is it, she wonders, that you're supposed to find something that isn't there? The pages don't turn backward. There's no word for that kind of love, in this language or any other.

THE MAGIC OF NEW YORK

Margaret Fuller
(1810–1850)

Margaret Fuller was one of the most brilliant and influential intellectuals of nineteenth-century America, a writer, critic and reformer whose work anticipated modern feminism. Born in Cambridge, Massachusetts, she became a central figure in the Transcendentalist movement, editing its journal *The Dial* and developing a formidable reputation as a conversationalist and essayist. Her most important book, *Woman in the Nineteenth Century* (1845), was a radical call for women's intellectual and political equality and quickly became a touchstone in debates about gender and democracy. In 1844, Fuller moved to New York City to serve as a literary critic for the *New-York Tribune*, becoming one of the first women in America to hold such a prominent journalistic role. In 1846, she left for Europe as a foreign correspondent and became directly involved in the revolutionary politics of Italy. Fuller's remarkable career was cut short at forty when she, her Italian partner and their young son drowned in a shipwreck off Fire Island in 1850. In this extract, her farewell column for the *Tribune*, Fuller reflects on her time in New York, suggesting the pace and possibility it presented to her 'could not be found in any other part of these United States'.

from Farewell

Farewell to New-York City, where twenty months have presented me with a richer and more varied exercise for thought and life than twenty years could in any other part of these United States.

It is the common remark about New-York that it has, at least, nothing petty or provincial in its methods and habits. The place is large enough; there is room enough and occupation enough for men to have no need or excuse for small cavils or scrutinies. A person who is independent and knows what he wants, may lead his proper life here unimpeded by others.

Vice and Crime, if flagrant and frequent, are less thickly coated by Hypocrisy than elsewhere. The air comes sometimes to the most infected subjects.

New-York is the focus, the point where American and European interests converge. There is no topic of general interest to men that will not betimes be brought before the thinker by the quick turning of the wheel.

Too quick that revolution, some object. Life rushes wide and free, but *too fast*; yet it is in the power of every one to avert from himself the evil that accompanies the good. He must build for his study, as did the German poet, a house beneath the bridge, and, then, all that passes above and by him will be heard and seen, but he will not be carried away with it.

Earlier views have been confirmed and many new

ones opened. On two great leadings,—the superlative importance of promoting National Education by heightening and deepening the cultivation of individual minds, and the part which is assigned to Woman in the next stage of human progress in this country, where most important achievements are to be effected, I have received much encouragement, much instruction, and the fairest hopes of more.

On various subjects of minor importance, no less than these. I hope for good results from observation with my own eyes of Life in the Old World, and to bring home some packages of seed for Life in the New.

Mark Twain
(1835–1910)

Mark Twain has been hailed as the father of American literature. His most famous novels – *The Adventures of Tom Sawyer* (1876) and *The Adventures of Huckleberry Finn* (1884) – were set along the Mississippi River, where he grew up, and blended vernacular speech with biting commentary on race and society. Twain's connections to New York City were, however, long and significant. He first arrived in the city aged seventeen, seeking work as a printer, and returned in the 1860s as a celebrated lecturer and correspondent, delighting large audiences at venues like Steinway Hall. After the death of his wife, he returned to New York, where from 1904 to 1908 he lived at 21 Fifth Avenue, not far from Washington Square. Always both charmed and appalled by the city's excesses, Twain cultivated a reputation as one of Manhattan's most colourful literary residents. He also worked with New York publishers throughout his career, and his sardonic wit found fertile ground in the city's bustling literary culture. In the two letters that follow, Twain makes a case for why General Ulysses S. Grant should be buried in New York rather than Washington DC, and writes to his daughter Clara about a memorable evening he spent in the city.

from Mark Twain's Letters

To the New York "Sun," on the proper place for Grant's Tomb:

TO THE EDITOR OF THE SUN:—SIR,—The newspaper atmosphere is charged with objections to New York as a place of sepulchre for General Grant, and the objectors are strenuous that Washington is the right place. They offer good reasons—good temporary reasons—for both of these positions.

But it seems to me that temporary reasons are not mete for the occasion. We need to consider posterity rather than our own generation. We should select a grave which will not merely be in the right place now, but will still be in the right place 500 years from now.

How does Washington promise as to that? You have only to hit it in one place to kill it. Some day the west will be numerically strong enough to move the seat of government; her past attempts are a fair warning that when the day comes she will do it. Then the city of Washington will lose its consequence and pass out of the public view and public talk. It is quite within the possibilities that, a century hence, people would wonder and say, "How did your predecessors come to bury their great dead in this deserted place?"

But as long as American civilization lasts New York will last. I cannot but think she has been well and wisely chosen as the guardian of a grave which is destined to become almost the most conspicuous in the world's history. Twenty centuries from now New York will still be New York, still a vast city, and the most notable object in it will still be the tomb and monument of General Grant.

I observe that the common and strongest objection to New York is that she is not "national ground." Let us give ourselves no uneasiness about that. Wherever General Grant's body lies, that is national ground.

S. L. CLEMENS.

To Clara Clemens, in Paris:

MR. ROGERS'S OFFICE, *FEB. 5, '94.*
Dear Benny—I was intending to answer your letter to-day, but I am away down town, and will simply whirl together a sentence or two for good-fellowship. I have bought photographs of Coquelin and Jane Hading and will ask them to sign them. I shall meet Coquelin tomorrow night, and if Hading is not present I will send her picture to her by somebody.

I am to breakfast with Madame Nordica in a few days, and meantime I hope to get a good picture of her to sign. She was of the breakfast company yesterday, but the picture of herself which she signed and gave me does not do her majestic beauty justice.

I am too busy to attend to the photo-collecting right, because I have to live up to the name which Jamie Dodge has given me—the "Belle of New York"—and it just keeps me rushing. Yesterday I had engagements to breakfast at noon, dine at 3, and dine again at 7. I got away from the long breakfast at 2 p. m., went and excused myself from the 3 o'clock dinner, then lunched with Mrs. Dodge in 58th street, returned to the Players and dressed, dined out at 7, and was back at Mrs. Dodge's at 10 p. m. where we had magic-lantern views of a superb sort, and a lot of yarns until an hour after midnight, and got to bed at 2 this morning—a good deal of a gain on my recent hours. But I don't get tired; I sleep as sound as a dead person, and always wake up fresh and strong—usually at exactly 9.

I was at breakfast lately where people of seven separate nationalities sat and the seven languages were going all the time. At my side sat a charming gentleman who was a delightful and active talker, and interesting. He talked glibly to those folks in all those seven languages—and still had a language to spare! I wanted to kill him, for very envy.

I greet you with love and kisses. PAPA.

Henry James
(1843–1916)

Henry James is best known for being a pre-eminent expatriate writer who penned some of the masterworks of nineteenth-century American fiction during the nearly four decades he spent living abroad in England. Many of his most famous novels – including *The Portrait of a Lady* (1881), *What Maisie Knew* (1897), *The Ambassadors* (1903) and *The Golden Bowl* (1904) – are set in Europe and turned an acute eye on what Americans and Europeans most miscalculate about each other. But he was a born New Yorker, and both his affection for his natal city and his ambivalence about the changes it underwent during his lifetime made their way into his fiction and essays. This extract, drawn from his 1907 collection of essays, *The American Scene*, about his recent return to and travels across the US, exults in the view of Hudson Bay and the power of the city as it plays out before him from his train carriage window as it enters New York.

from The American Scene

The single impression or particular vision most answering to the greatness of the subject would have been, I think, a certain hour of large circumnavigation that I found prescribed, in the fulness of the spring, as the almost immediate crown of a return from the Far West. I had arrived at one of the transpontine stations of the Pennsylvania Railroad; the question was of proceeding to Boston, for the occasion, without pushing through the terrible town—why "terrible," to my sense, in many ways, I shall presently explain—and the easy and agreeable attainment of this great advantage was to embark on one of the mightiest (as appeared to me) of train-bearing barges and, descending the western waters, pass round the bottom of the city and remount the other current to Harlem; all without "losing touch" of the Pullman that had brought me from Washington. This absence of the need of losing touch, this breadth of effect, as to the whole process, involved in the prompt floating of the huge concatenated cars not only without arrest or confusion, but as for positive prodigal beguilement of the artless traveller, had doubtless much to say to the ensuing state of mind, the happily-excited and amused view of the great face of New York. The extent, the ease, the energy, the quantity and number, all notes scattered about as if, in the whole business and in the splendid light, nature and science were joyously romping together, might have been taking on again, for their symbol, some collective presence of great circling and plunging, hovering and perching seabirds, white-winged images of the spirit, of the restless freedom of the Bay. The Bay had always, on other opportunities, seemed to blow its immense character straight into one's face—coming "at" you, so to speak, bearing down on you, with the full force of a thousand prows of steamers seen exactly on the line of their longitudinal axis; but I had never before been so conscious of its boundless cool assurance or seemed to see its genius so grandly at play. This was presumably indeed because I had never before enjoyed the remarkable adventure of taking in so much of the vast bristling promontory from the water, of ascending the East River, in especial, to its upper diminishing expanses.

Something of the air of the occasion and of the mood of the moment caused the whole picture to speak with its largest suggestion; which suggestion is irresistible when once it is sounded clear. It is all, absolutely, an expression of things lately and currently *done,* done on a large impersonal stage and on the basis of inordinate gain—it is not an expression of any other matters whatever; and yet the sense of the scene (which had at several previous junctures, as well, put forth to my imagination its power) was commanding and thrilling, was in certain lights almost charming. So it befell, exactly, that an element of mystery and wonder entered into the impression—the interest of trying to make out, in the absence of features of the sort usually supposed indispensable, the reason of the beauty and the joy. It is indubitably a "great" bay, a great harbour, but no one item of the romantic, or even of the picturesque, as commonly understood, contributes to its effect. The shores are low and for the most part depressingly furnished and prosaically peopled; the islands, though numerous, have not a grace to exhibit, and one thinks of the other, the real flowers of geography in this order, of Naples, of Capetown, of Sydney, of Seattle, of San Francisco, of Rio, asking how if *they* justify a reputation, New York should seem to justify one. Then, after all, we remember that there are reputations and reputations; we remember above all that the imaginative response to the conditions here presented may just happen to proceed from the intellectual extravagance of the given observer. When this personage is open to corruption by almost any large view of an intensity of life, his vibrations tend to become a matter difficult even for *him* to explain. He may have to confess that the group of evident facts fails to account by itself for the complacency of his appreciation. Therefore it is that I find myself rather backward with a perceived sanction, of an at all proportionate kind, for the fine exhilaration with which, in this free wayfaring relation to them, the wide waters of New York inspire me. There is the beauty of light and air, the great scale of space, and, seen far away to the west, the open gates of the Hudson, majestic in their degree, even at a distance, and announcing still nobler things. But the real appeal, unmistakably, is in that note of vehemence in the local life of which I have spoken, for it is the appeal of a particular type of dauntless power.

The aspect the power wears then is indescribable; it is the power of the most extravagant of cities, rejoicing, as with the voice of the morning, in its might, its fortune, its unsurpassable conditions, and imparting to every object and element, to the motion and expression of every floating, hurrying, panting thing, to the throb of ferries and tugs, to the plash of waves and the play of winds and the glint of lights and the shrill of whistles and the quality and authority of breeze-borne cries—all, practically, a diffused, wasted clamour of *detonations*—something of its sharp free accent and, above all, of its sovereign sense of being "backed" and able to back. The universal *applied* passion struck me as shining unprecedentedly out of the composition; in the bigness and bravery and insolence, especially, of everything that rushed and shrieked; in the air as of a great intricate frenzied dance, half merry, half desperate, or at least half defiant, performed on the huge watery floor. This appearance of the bold lacing-together, across the waters, of the scattered members of the monstrous organism—lacing as by the ceaseless play of an enormous system of steam-shuttles or electric bobbins (I scarce know what to call them), commensurate in form with their infinite work—does perhaps more than anything else to give the pitch of the vision of energy. One has the sense that the monster grows and grows, flinging abroad its loose limbs even as some unmannered young giant at his "larks," and that the binding stitches must for ever fly further and faster and draw harder; the future complexity of the web, all under the sky and over the sea, becoming thus that of some colossal set of clockworks, some steel-souled machine-room of brandished arms and hammering fists and opening and closing jaws. The immeasurable bridges are but as the horizontal sheaths of pistons working at high pressure, day and night, and subject, one apprehends with perhaps inconsistent gloom, to certain, to fantastic, to merciless multiplication. In the light of this apprehension indeed the breezy brightness of the Bay puts on the semblance of the vast white page that awaits beyond any other perhaps the black overscoring of science.

Djuna Barnes
(1892–1982)

Djuna Barnes was an extraordinarily original American writer, journalist and playwright whose avant-garde work explored sexuality, gender and art with daring intensity. Although she is now best remembered for landmark modernist works such as *Nightwood*, written during her many years in Paris, she got her start as a writer when she moved to Greenwich Village in 1912. As a young journalist she contributed to New York newspapers and magazines, including the *Brooklyn Daily Eagle* and *Vanity Fair*, often writing first-person 'stunt' pieces and interviews. Like many writers of her generation, she headed to Paris in the 1920s, where she joined a vibrant community of writers and artists. After her return to New York in 1940, Barnes lived in near seclusion at 5 Patchin Place in Greenwich Village for over forty years, continuing to write but publishing little. Though she shunned publicity, her reputation steadily grew, and by the 1970s she was revered by a new generation of feminist and queer writers and critics for her groundbreaking writings. In this essay, 'Why Go Abroad?', published in the *Brooklyn Daily Eagle* in 1913, Barnes sketches the sounds, bustle, foods and colour of Brooklyn's Wallabout Market, suggesting for readers that all of Europe can be found there.

Why Go Abroad? See Europe in Brooklyn!

Three thousand miles away, on a foreign shore, pictured to us in the graphic language of men who went and saw, and, seeing, wrote; painted for us by dreamers who unite conception with oil; dwelt on by us as something yet to realize, of its sorrow, of its charm, of its serenity; of its splendor of color, united with splendor of line; of the splendor of little things and the splendor of great—this is the land of our hearts. We are going to it when we have saved enough; some day when the teapot bank can hold no more, or some day when our uncles decide to rent a seat in ether, when we are grown. This is the land that is swarming with incidents and is profligate with gasps. We are even now in the throes of the mental shiver of expectancy.

And yet we have opportunity, we stay-at-home, to go down to it and see it for ourselves. How many of us have discovered it? Just how many know that Europe is in Brooklyn?

Wallabout! Wallabout! Wallabout! Why in the world haven't you sensed it? Here you can see the colored quilt that covers a spavined horse, the tambourine that receives the proceeds of a soul in that soul's metal; music which brings forth a dime or an onion from the listeners in the shops.

Why, oh, why, my feet, have you not dodged the pungent, omnipotent pepper, the crescendo of screaming peanuts roasting, the howl of the hucksters and the background of tired, silent horses ruminating in the sunset?

Over this presides the genius of Time, represented by the clock in the market square, in the tower house where sits the market clerk over his ledger counting up the quarters he has collected from the farmer for standing rent in the aisles of the square. As its hands come around toward 5 you know that the few who are widest awake are due. Between the clock and the restaurant abutting, with tall glasses of spaghetti and crushed brown figs, hangs a low, swinging, lax line of clothes beating a flapping tatoo upon the blug of an awakening sky. Giuseppi grew up to its tune. The clock and the stores and the streets and the very city itself he has learned to sense by smell, as he handles his bananas. Giuseppi soaked in it, no longer knows that his very coat tails spell Florida; that his floating tie and his rakish, bagging shirt all are weaved with the flax of fruit.

Life is changing, but Wallabout goes on, stark calm in the gray of a winter dawn. Night is pierced by an upward thrust chimney which smokes in great lazy gasps; low boats purr in the harbor and the wet canvas flaps upon a wet deck and there is the spray and the rime and the tumult of the sea, and then the dusk lifts and the houses become buildings and the windows and doors take form and the cobbles come into existence as slowly stealing in from the forty roads of produce, the horses come. Carts piled to the point of satisfaction with cabbages and turnips and beets, and upon the seats, their heads upon their breasts, the Long Island farmers sleep as they bring our dinner in.

From the hold of the dusky boats that murmured in the dawn come the imports, the grapes, the nuts, the figs, up from the sheltering decks, hauled and cursed over by men in open shirts and dirt colored trousers. So comes our dessert.

And then we must sing of the "multi-gan," that brews in the pot of our little Italy, that pot of soup that simmers upon the hob in some humble home; that lyrical street-gathered mulligan, gleaned by women in monstrously tucked skirts and enveloping shawls, caught at with furtive eyes, for even though it is not forbidden, the getting makes it sweet.

By twelve the market must be clear of carts; and rubbish men and women make room for the street cleaners, who gather up anything that may have been overlooked. The square has to be cleaned for the night renting, when the 6 o'clock loads come in. The commission merchant has got through handling the beets and the cauliflower and the beans and the celery. He has put his price on the load as it stands, and he has already by 12, disposed of it all to the merchants of the market. He folds his hands and loiters about waiting for the next line, and the marketeers handle the goods and smell of the fruits and count up their profit and their loss and never seem to know that they have been done out of so many cents to the pound by a few yards, for these Long Island farmers stand within a block of their markets and yet they wait for the commission merchant to buy first.

Every bit of broken box is reduced to kindling and run off with by bare-legged boys with their soap-box carts, every hoop and every nail and every scrap of paper is likewise collected and the busy mother stands behind and goads with little hissing foreign curses and menacing circles of the arm.

Life, bustle, color, Europe, barter, gain, loss, Wallabout, Wallabout, Wallabout, somebody, anybody, something is here to be learned. No trip to the foreign land is needed, if it's atmosphere you want. No need is there to stifle in the body of a ship for six or seven days, if it's accent you want. No need to count the money in the teapot if it's movement and music that you seek. The organ grinder with his tambourine-beating wife, wedges between the crowds and receives in the soul's metal, a dime or an onion.

DOROTHY PARKER
(1893–1967)

Dorothy Parker was a poet, critic, screenwriter and satirist whose wit made her one of the most quoted literary voices of the twentieth century. Raised on Manhattan's Upper West Side, she began her career as a journalist, writing for *Vogue* and *Vanity Fair* before becoming a founding contributor to *The New Yorker* and gaining fame as a member of the Algonquin Round Table, a celebrated circle of writers, critics and actors. Parker published several acclaimed poetry collections, including *Enough Rope* (1926), *Sunset Gun* (1928) and *Death and Taxes* (1931), as well as short stories and screenplays. Her trademark humour was always tempered by social conscience: she helped found the Screen Writers' Guild, was active in left-wing politics and faced blacklisting during the McCarthy era. Though she spent much of her later life in California, Parker remained indelibly identified with New York, the city whose ironies and heartbreak she captured so well. At her death in 1967, her ashes were interred at the NAACP headquarters in Baltimore but later moved to Woodlawn Cemetery in the Bronx. In this delightful extract from 'My Hometown', first published in *McCall's Magazine*, Parker spells out her irrepressible love for New York, that city she calls her own.

from My Hometown

It is sentimental or presumptuous or too, too whimsical, according to the way you look at it, but my feeling for New York is maternal. I know it is a bad, head-strong, selfish brat, and will undoubtedly let me die in the poorhouse; I know its manners are, at best, but company ones, and its ways have been picked up from no companions of my choosing; I have for it all the futile exasperation of the clinging, jealous, bewildered mother. I know its faults, backward and forward and all around. And nobody but me is going to say anything about them while I am in the room!

You see, I have always lived in New York. I was cheated out of the distinction of being a native New Yorker, because I had to go and get born while the family was spending the Summer in New Jersey, but, honestly, we came back into town right after Labor Day, so I nearly made the grade. And as a matter of fact, the rarity of native New Yorkers is but one of our island myths; I know at least four personally, and I have a good chance, if things go right, of meeting two others. When I was a little girl—which was along about the time that practically nobody was safe from Indians—I was insular beyond belief. At Summer resorts, I would ask my new playmates "What street do you live on?" I never said "What town do you live in?" I admit that that is the spirit that estranges the Mrs. Whittakers.

I am not like that any more. It occurs to me that there are other towns. It occurs to me so violently that I say, at intervals, "Very well, if New York is going to be like this, I'm going to live somewhere else." And I do—that's the funny part of it. But then one day there comes to me the sharp picture of New York at its best, on a shiny, blue-and-white Autumn day with its buildings cut diagonally in halves of light and shadow, with its straight, neat avenues colored with quick throngs, like confetti in a breeze. Some one, and I wish it had been I, has said that "Autumn is the Springtime of big cities." I see New York at holiday time, always in the late afternoon, under a Maxfield Parish sky, with the crowds even more quick and nervous but even more good-natured, the dark groups splashed with the white of Christmas packages, the lighted, holly-strung shops urging them in to buy more and more. I see it on a Spring morning, with the clothes of the women as soft and as hopeful as the pretty new leaves on a few, brave trees. I see it at night, with the low skies red with the back-flung lights of Broadway, those lights of which Chesterton—or they told me it was Chesterton—said, "What a marvelous sight for those who cannot read!" I see it in the rain, I smell the enchanting odor of wet asphalt, with the empty streets black and shining as ripe olives. I see it—by this time, I become maudlin with nostalgia—even with its gray mounds of crusted snow, its little Appalachians of ice along the pavements. So I go back. And it is always better than I thought it would be.

I suppose that is the thing about New York. It is always a little more than you had hoped for. Each day, there, is so definitely a new day. "Now we'll start all over," it seems to say every morning, "and come on, let's hurry like anything."

London is satisfied, Paris is resigned, but New York is always hopeful. Always it believes that something particularly good is about to come off, and it must hurry to meet it. There is excitement ever running its streets. Each day, as you go out, you feel the little nervous quiver that is yours when you sit in a theater just before the curtain rises. Other places may give you a sweet and soothing sense of level; but in New York there is always the feeling of "Something's going to happen." It isn't peace. But, you know, you do get used to peace, and so quickly. And you never get used to New York.

HELEN KELLER
(1880–1968)

Helen Keller, deaf and blind from infancy, became one of the most admired public figures of the twentieth century, celebrated around the globe for her writing, lectures and advocacy on behalf of people with disabilities. With the help of her teacher, Anne Sullivan, Keller famously learned to communicate, eventually graduating from Radcliffe College in 1904. Her first autobiography, *The Story of My Life* (1903), remains a classic of American literature, subsequently adapted as a Tony Award-winning Broadway play in 1959 and acclaimed Hollywood film in 1962. She spent two decades in New York City, living from 1917 to 1938 at 93 Seminole Avenue in Forest Hills, Queens, and working closely with the American Foundation for the Blind, headquartered in Manhattan. Her office there became a hub for her worldwide activism, which linked disability rights to broader struggles for equality, economic justice and peace. In 1920, she helped to found the American Civil Liberties Union, still headquartered in New York. In this evocative excerpt drawn from her 1929 memoir, *Midstream: My Later Life*, Keller offers us a thrilling taste of New York City – a walk along its streets and a ride on one of its subway cars – as a remarkable sensory symphony of smells, sounds and tactile experiences.

from Midstream: My Later Life

I usually know what part of the city I am in by the odours. There are as many smells as there are philosophies. I have never had time to gather and classify my olfactory impressions of different cities, but it would be an interesting subject. I find it quite natural to think of places by their characteristic smells.

Fifth Avenue, for example, has a different odour from any other part of New York or elsewhere. Indeed, it is a very odorous street. It may sound like a joke to say that it has an aristocratic smell; but it has, nevertheless. As I walk along its even pavements, I recognize expensive perfumes, powders, creams, choice flowers, and pleasant exhalations from the houses. In the residential section I smell delicate food, silken draperies, and rich tapestries. Sometimes, when a door opens as I pass, I know what kind of cosmetics the occupants of the house use. I know if there is an open fire, if they burn wood or soft coal, if they roast their coffee, if they use candles, if the house has been shut up for a long time, if it has been painted or newly decorated, and if the cleaners are at work in it. I suggest that if the police really wish to know where stills and "speakeasies" are located, they take me with them. It would not be a bad idea for the United States Government to establish a bureau of aromatic specialists.

New York has a special interest for me when it is

wrapped in fog. Then it behaves very much like a blind person. I once crossed from Jersey City to Manhattan in a dense fog. The ferry-boat felt its way cautiously through the river traffic. More timid than a blind man, its horn brayed incessantly. Fog-bound, surrounded by menacing, unseen craft and dangers, it halted every now and then as a blind man halts at a crowded thoroughfare crossing, tapping his cane, tense and anxious.

As I walk up Broadway, the people that brush past me seem always hastening toward a destination they never reach. Their motions are eager, as if they said, "We are on our way, we shall arrive in a moment." They keep up the pace—they almost run. Each on his quest intent, in endless procession they pass, tragic, grotesque, gay, they all sweep onward like rain falling upon leaves. I wonder where they are going. I puzzle my brain; but the mystery is never solved. Will they at last come somewhere? Will anybody be waiting for them? The march never ceases. Their feet have worn the pavements unevenly. I wish I knew where they are going. Some are nonchalant, some walk with their eyes on the ground, others step lightly, as if they might fly if their wings were not bound by the multitude. A pale little woman is guiding the steps of a blind man. His great hand drags on her arm. Awkwardly he shortens his stride to her gait. He trips when the curb is uneven; his grip tightens on the arm of the woman. Where are they going?

Like figures in a meaningless pageant, they pass. There are young girls laughing, loitering. They have beauty, youth, lovers. They look in the shop windows, they look at the huge winking signs; they jostle the crowds, their feet keep time to the music of their hearts. They must be going to a pleasant place. I think I should like to go where they are going.

Tremulously I stand in the subways, absorbed into the terrible reverberations of exploding energy. Fearful, I touch the forest of steel girders loud with the thunder of oncoming trains that shoot past me like projectiles. Inert I stand, riveted in my place. My limbs, paralyzed, refuse to obey the will insistent on haste to board the train while the lightning steed is leashed and its reeling speed checked for a moment. Before my mind flashes in clairvoyant vision what all this speed portends—the lightning crashing into life, the accidents, railroad wrecks, steam bursting free like geysers from bands of steel, thousands of racing motors and children caught at play, flying heroes diving into the sea, dying for speed—all this because of strange, unsatisfied ambitions. Another train bursts into the station like a volcano, the people crowd me on, on into the chasm—into the dark depths of awful forces and fates. In a few minutes, still trembling, I am spilled into the streets.

Permissions Acknowledgements

'Lennox Avenue: Midnight' from *The Collected Poems of Langston Hughes* (Alfred A. Knopf Inc), reproduced by permission of David Higham Associates Ltd.

'A Trip on Staten Island Ferry' from *The Collected Poems of Audre Lorde* (W. W. Norton, New York), © 1997 by the estate of Audre Lorde. Used with permission from the Abner Stein Agency.

Extract from *A Time to Be Born* by Dawn Powell reproduced with permission of Pushkin Press, on behalf of the Literary Executors of the Estate of Dawn Powell. Copyright 1942 © Dawn Powell.

'Invitation to Miss Marianne Moore' from *Poems* by Elizabeth Bishop. Copyright © 2011 by The Alice H. Methfessel Trust. Compilation copyright © 2011 by Farrar, Straus and Giroux. Reprinted by permission of Farrar, Straus and Giroux in the US and by The Random House Group Limited in the UK. All rights reserved.

Extract from *Brown Girl, Brownstones* © Paule Marshall 1956. Reproduced by kind permission of the Marshall family.

'My Sad Self' by Allen Ginsberg. Copyright © "My Sad Self" from *Collected Poems, 1947–1980* © 1984 by Allen Ginsberg, used by permission of The Wylie Agency (UK) Limited.

'My Sad Self' from *The Collected Poems: 1947–1997* by Allen Ginsberg. Copyright © 2006 by the Allen Ginsberg Trust. Used by permission of HarperCollins Publishers.

Anaïs Nin letter to Henry Miller (3 December 1934) from *A Literate Passion: Letters of Anaïs Nin & Henry Miler, 1932–1953*. Copyright © 1987 by Rupert Pole, as Trustee under the Last Will and Testament of Anaïs Nin. Used by permission of HarperCollins Publishers and the Anaïs Nin Foundation.

Extract from 'Nobody Ever Gets Lost' copyright © 2011 by Jess Row.

'Why Go Abroad?' by Djuna Barnes used with permission from the Authors League Fund and St Bride's Church, joint literary executors of the Estate of Djuna Barnes.

Macmillan Collector's Library wishes to thank the NAACP Empowerment Programs, Inc., the copyright owner of Dorothy Parker's literary estate, for the use of 'My Hometown' by Dorothy Parker, first published in *McCall's Magazine* in January 1928.

Extracts from *Midstream: My Later Life* by Helen Keller first published in 1929. Macmillan Collector's Library acknowledges the American Foundation for the Blind as the steward of the Helen Keller Archive.

MACMILLAN COLLECTOR'S LIBRARY

Own the world's great works of literature in one beautiful collectible library

Designed and curated to appeal to book lovers everywhere, Macmillan Collector's Library editions are small enough to travel with you and striking enough to take pride of place on your bookshelf. These much-loved literary classics also make the perfect gift.

Beautifully made, every Macmillan Collector's Library book adheres to the same high production values. Each hardback features gilt edges, a ribbon marker and cloth binding, and every paperback has a bespoke illustrated cover.

Discover a new and exciting anthology or cherish your favourite classic stories with this elegant collection.

Macmillan Collector's Library: own, collect, and treasure

Discover the full range at
panmacmillan.com/mcl